Free the Worms!

by Nancy Krulik • illustrated by John & Wendy

Grosset & Dunlap

For Sarah and Emily—N.K.
For Judy—friend of the little guy!—J&W

GROSSET & DUNLAP
Published by the Penguin Group
Penguin Group (USA) Inc., 375 Hudson Street, New York, New York 10014, USA
Penguin Group (Canada), 90 Eglinton Avenue East, Suite 700, Toronto,
Ontario M4P 2Y3, Canada
(a division of Pearson Penguin Canada Inc.)
Penguin Books Ltd., 80 Strand, London WC2R 0RL, England
Penguin Group Ireland, 25 St. Stephen's Green, Dublin 2, Ireland
(a division of Penguin Books Ltd.)
Penguin Group (Australia), 250 Camberwell Road, Camberwell,
Victoria 3124, Australia
(a division of Pearson Australia Group Pty. Ltd.)
Penguin Books India Pvt. Ltd., 11 Community Centre, Panchsheel Park,
New Delhi—110 017, India
Penguin Group (NZ), 67 Apollo Drive, Rosedale, North Shore 0632, New Zealand
(a division of Pearson New Zealand Ltd.)
Penguin Books (South Africa) (Pty.) Ltd., 24 Sturdee Avenue,
Rosebank, Johannesburg 2196, South Africa

Penguin Books Ltd., Registered Offices: 80 Strand, London WC2R 0RL, England

Text copyright © 2008 by Nancy Krulik. Illustrations copyright © 2008
by John and Wendy. All rights reserved. Published by Grosset & Dunlap, a
division of Penguin Young Readers Group, 345 Hudson Street, New York, New
York 10014. GROSSET & DUNLAP is a trademark of Penguin Group (USA) Inc.
Printed in the U.S.A.

Library of Congress Control Number: 2007034406

ISBN 978-0-448-44675-2   10 9 8 7 6 5 4 3 2 1

Chapter 1

"Ruff! Ruff!"

Katie Carew watched as her chocolate-and-white cocker spaniel, Pepper, jumped up and down near the tree in her backyard. He was barking at a gray squirrel on a branch above.

"Ruff! Ruff!" Pepper barked louder.

The squirrel opened its mouth and let an acorn drop. *Clunk.* It hit Pepper right on the head.

"Aroooo!" Pepper howled. He jumped up again.

Clunk. Down came another acorn. This one hit Pepper on the rear end.

That did it! "ARROOOOOO! RUFFFF! ARF!"

Pepper was barking *really* loud now!

"He wants to get that squirrel," Katie's friend Emma Weber said as the two girls watched Pepper leaping up and down on his hind legs.

Katie nodded. "But he won't catch him. He never does. It's just this game they play."

"He looks like he's having fun, though," Emma said.

Katie grinned. Pepper definitely seemed happy. His stubby little tail was wagging back and forth so fast, it looked like a brown blur.

"Arooo! Arf!" Pepper barked at the squirrel. He leaped up and down against the tree trunk.

"It's just that he's hard to draw when he's jumping," Emma told Katie. "He's not a very cooperative model."

"I know. All I've been able to draw is his ear," Katie agreed, looking down at her drawing pad. "The only time Pepper sits still is when he's asleep."

"Your dog is a lot like my twin brothers," Emma said.

Katie knew what she meant. Emma's twin brothers, Tyler and Timmy, were only a year old. They had just learned to walk. Now they never seemed to want to sit still. They were always getting into messes. Just like Pepper.

"Hey, look!" Emma exclaimed, pointing to the tree branch. "Now there are *three* squirrels up there. And they're all throwing acorns at Pepper."

"Three against one. That's not fair!" Katie shouted up at the squirrels.

The squirrels ignored her completely.

"Come on, Emma!" Katie said, dropping her paper and crayons and running over to the tree.

"What are we doing?" Emma asked.

"We're going to be on Pepper's team," Katie told her. She dropped down on all fours and started barking like a dog. "Ruff! Ruff!"

Emma grinned. She got down on all fours, too. "Arrooooo!" she howled.

"Arf! Arf!" Pepper barked.

"Ruff!" Katie barked. Then she wiggled her

rear end. "Look, I'm wagging my tail," she told Emma.

Emma dropped down onto her belly. Then she flipped over onto her back.

"What are you doing?" Katie asked her.

"I'm rolling over," Emma told her.

Katie laughed and rolled over in the grass, too.

"Animals have all the fun," Emma said.

"They really do," Katie agreed. "Nobody ever yells at them for getting dirty."

Emma wriggled out of her sweater, which had leaves and mud stuck on it. "Now I'm a snake. Get it?"

"Yes! Just like Slinky." Their class was learning about reptiles. Snakes like their class pet, Slinky, shed their old skin. Then there was a clean new skin underneath.

Katie got down on her belly and began slithering around in the grass. "Look at me! I'm a snake, too!" she told Emma.

Clunk. Just then another acorn fell from

the tree. This one hit Katie on the arm. She looked up.

The three squirrels were sitting up there. They almost seemed as if they were laughing at her.

"That's it!" Katie exclaimed, leaping back up onto all fours. "Come on, Emma. Let's be dogs again. Pepper needs all the help he can get!"

"Arff!" Emma barked.

"Aroo!" Katie howled.

"Grrrr ruff! Ruff!" Pepper growled.

That was enough to scare the three squirrels out of the tree. They leaped onto a nearby fence, and ran out of the yard.

"Victory!" Emma shouted.

"Arooooo!" Pepper howled happily.

"Yes, Pepper. You're right. Dogs rule!" Katie cheered.

Chapter 2

"This is the best vegetarian chili I've ever eaten," Emma W. told Katie's mom later that evening. She stopped for a second and thought. "It's also the *only* vegetarian chili I've ever eaten."

"Vegetarian lasagna is yummy, too," Katie told Emma. "Oh, and veggie burgers. I love when Daddy makes those on the grill."

"Don't forget the grilled vegetables I pile on top of them," Mr. Carew proudly reminded Katie.

"Is it hard being a vegetarian?" Emma asked Katie.

Katie shook her head. "No. It's easy. I've

been a vegetarian for a long time."

"How come?" Emma asked her.

"I just don't want to eat anything that ever had a face," Katie explained. "I guess I stopped eating meat right around the time we adopted Pepper from the animal shelter."

At the sound of his name, Pepper came running over. He plopped himself down beside Katie and looked up, hopefully.

"I think Pepper wishes he had some of this people food," Emma said.

Katie gulped. "He does not!" she insisted. "He doesn't wish that at all!"

Everyone at the table stopped eating and stared at her. Katie turned beet red. She knew they all thought she was acting weird.

But it was just that Katie hated wishes.

It all started back in third grade on one terrible, horrible day. Katie had missed the football and lost the game for her team. Then she'd fallen in a big mud puddle and ruined her favorite pair of jeans. Even worse, she'd let out a huge burp in front of the whole class. How embarrassing!

That night, Katie had wished she could be anyone but herself. There must have been a shooting star overhead or something, because the next day the magic wind came.

The magic wind was a super-strong, tornado-like wind that blew only around Katie. It was so powerful that every time it came, it turned Katie into someone else.

The first time the magic wind came it turned Katie into Speedy, the class 3A hamster. After escaping from the cage, she wound up inside George's stinky sneaker. YUCK! Luckily, the magic wind had returned to switcheroo Katie back into a kid again, before anyone realized that she'd been running around the school—with nothing on but hamster fur!

The magic wind followed Katie everywhere she went—even all the way to Europe. When Katie was in England on vacation, the wind turned her into a guard at Buckingham Palace.

Those guards are trained not to smile no matter what the people around them are doing. But Katie wasn't trained for anything. And she didn't just smile. She burst out laughing—and got the poor guard she'd turned into fired!

Then there was the time the magic wind turned Katie into Pepper. She'd accidentally

broken a statue in her next-door neighbor's yard.

After that Pepper had to be on a leash if he wanted to walk anywhere! That wasn't very fair, since it was actually Katie who had caused the mess. Of course, Katie was the only one who knew that, so no one suggested she be put on a leash to go for a walk!

That was the biggest problem with the magic wind. It always blew in trouble. Then it was up to Katie to make things right again.

The magic wind was the reason Katie never made wishes anymore. But of course she couldn't explain that to Emma W. and her parents. They wouldn't believe her, anyway. Katie wouldn't have believed it herself if it didn't keep happening to her.

Still, she knew she had to say something, and *fast*.

"Um . . . I just mean Pepper is better off with *his* food," Katie told them. "This chili would be too spicy for him."

"That's true," Katie's dad said. "Dog food is the best thing for dogs."

"But people eat different foods every day," Emma W. insisted, "and all he gets is the same old doggie kibble in his bowl."

"Oh, I can fix that," Katie told her. She got up from the table and walked over to the cabinet where the dog food was kept. She pulled out a green bone-shaped doggie cookie.

"Pepper, treat!" she called out.

Pepper knew what that meant. He raced over to Katie, his little tail wagging.

"Sit," Katie said.

Pepper sat.

"Give paw," Katie said.

Pepper lifted up his right front paw.

Katie shook his furry hand. "Good boy," she praised her dog. Then she gave him the cookie.

Pepper swallowed it up in one gulp. Then he let out a little bark.

"You're welcome," Katie said with a giggle.

"How did you know he said 'thank you'?"

Emma asked her.

Katie smiled. "Oh, I just *think* I know what it's like to be a dog. Isn't that right, Pepper?"

"Aarf!" Pepper agreed.

Chapter 3

"Katie Kazoo, you gotta hear about this!" George Brennan shouted the next morning as Katie arrived at the school playground.

Katie grinned when she heard George using the way-cool nickname he'd given her last year. She loved the way it sounded.

"What's up?" Katie asked him.

"I'm gonna be a rock star!" George told her. "And so are Jeremy and Kevin. We're starting a band. I'm going to be the keyboard player."

"But you don't play the keyboards," Katie reminded him. "You play the tuba in beginning band."

George shook his head. "Not anymore. There aren't tubas in rock bands. So I'm switching. Kevin's switching, too, from trumpet to guitar. Mr. Starkey said it would be okay."

Katie nodded. Mr. Starkey was the band teacher. If he said it was okay, it must be. "But Jeremy's still playing drums, right?" Katie asked him.

George nodded. "You need drums if you're going to have a really rocking band."

Just then, Kevin Camilleri and Jeremy Fox—the other two boys in the band—walked over. Jeremy made two fists and began to drum in the air. Kevin played air guitar.

"Rock on, dudes!" Kevin exclaimed.

"Rock on!" Jeremy and George shouted back. Then they all went back to playing their imaginary instruments.

"What are you guys doing?" Suzanne Lock asked as she walked over to the group.

"Did you hear the news?" Katie asked her.

Suzanne scrunched up her mouth and

squinted slightly.
"What news?" she
asked kind of angrily.

Katie knew why
Suzanne was upset.
She hated it when
anyone found things out before she did. And
this time Katie was the one with the info.

"These guys have started a band!" Katie
exclaimed.

Suzanne looked over at the boys. George was still moving his fingers back and forth across his imaginary keyboard. Jeremy was drumming on nothing, and Kevin was rocking out on air guitar.

"They sound great," she joked.

"No, seriously," Katie said. "George is going to play keyboards, Jeremy is going to play drums, and Kevin is going to play guitar." She looked at the expression on Suzanne's face. "*Real* ones," Katie insisted.

"But they don't know how to play those instruments," Suzanne said.

"We're going to start taking lessons," Kevin told her.

"A fourth-grade rock band," Katie said. "It's going to be so cool."

"Do you want to join?" Jeremy asked her. "Maybe you could play bass guitar or something."

Katie smiled. Jeremy was a really great friend. He always tried to include her. But this time, Katie wasn't interested. "I think I'll stick with the clarinet," she told him. "I'm getting pretty good."

"Yeah, I heard you at beginning band practice," Jeremy agreed. "You sounded great on 'This Old Man.'"

"We're not going to play any of those old songs," George told her. "We're doing new, *rocking* songs."

"Our first single is going to be 'Lizard Rock,'" Kevin said. "We wrote the beginning of it on the phone last night."

"Lizard on a rock, listening to rock. Rock on!" the boys all sang at once. "That reptile's gone wild. Rock on!"

"That was deep," Suzanne said sarcastically.

"*I* liked it!" Katie exclaimed.

"Thanks," Jeremy told Katie. "We got the idea for it from studying reptiles."

"I figured," Katie said. "It's awesome. You guys can count on me to be your biggest fan.

And I want you to give me your autographs right now. Who knows? Someday you might be famous!"

Chapter 4

Katie walked into class 4A and sat right down in her beanbag chair. All of the kids in class 4A sat in beanbags. Katie's teacher, Mr. Guthrie, thought kids learned better when they were comfortable.

For Katie, the best part of having a beanbag chair was that the kids got to decorate them every time they had a new learning adventure. (That's what Mr. G. called lessons.)

Right now they were studying reptiles. So Katie had decorated her beanbag to look like a gecko—with a long green crepe-paper tail, brown and green construction-paper scales, and feet made of green felt.

Emma W. had decorated hers to look like a tortoise.

Emma Stavros had made hers look like a brown-and-white desert iguana.

Mandy Banks had turned hers into an amazing Komodo dragon lizard.

Kadeem Carter's was a rainbow-colored chameleon.

George and Kevin were sitting in matching crocodile beanbags.

And Andrew Epstein had created an alligator, which looked a lot like George and Kevin's crocodiles, but with a wider snout.

No doubt about it. Class 4A was Reptile World. But that was nothing new. All year long, Class 4A had been Slinky the snake's home.

As far as Katie was concerned, Slinky was the coolest pet in the whole school. Lots of classes had guinea pigs, hamsters, and gerbils in their rooms. But 4A was the only class with their very own snake.

"Okay, dudes," Mr. G. said, once all the kids

were seated. "Time for that awesome creative-writing assignment I promised you yesterday."

Katie sat up tall in her lizard beanbag. She loved any kind of assignment that was creative. Especially the ones Mr. G. came up with.

"I want you each to write a poem," Mr. G. continued. "And not just any poem. I want you to write a poem about reptiles."

Katie frowned. That was a tough one. Usually, she liked to write poems with words that rhymed. But what rhymed with *lizard? Gizzard? Schnizzard?*

And what about *gecko? Let go?* Not exactly.

Tortoise? Well that sort of rhymed with *porpoise.* Except not really. And porpoises weren't reptiles, anyway.

Katie's eyes drifted over to where Slinky the snake was lying in his cage. That was it! Katie would write a poem about the class snake. Lots of things rhymed with snake! She opened her notebook to a clean page and began to write.

SLINKY THE SNAKE

By Katie Carew

We saw an eggshell break,

And out came Slinky the snake.

So you could say maybe

He's our little baby.

He crawls on his belly

He's not slimy or smelly.

His skin has scales

To grip trees and rails.

Scales keep water out, too,

Like our raincoats do.

He's the best pet in school

I think snakes rule!

When she was finished, Katie read her poem from top to bottom. It was almost perfect. Except for one thing. Katie wanted to draw a picture of Slinky to go with the poem.

Katie looked over at the snake. He was lying quietly in his cage.

He'll be a lot easier to draw than Pepper, she thought happily.

But before Katie could pull out her colored pencils, Mr. G. clapped his hands. "Okay, dudes!" he exclaimed. "Finish up. We're going outside."

"Cool!" Kevin exclaimed.

"What are we going to do out there?" George asked.

"That's for me to know and you to find out," Mr. G. told him. "So line up!"

Katie closed her writer's notebook. What in the world could Mr. G.'s latest surprise be?

Chapter 5

"Okay, gang, here's the deal. We're going worm hunting," Mr. G. told the kids.

"What?" several kids shouted.

"You heard me. I want you to catch worms."

"What for?" Kadeem Carter asked.

"You'll find out in just a little while," Mr. G. told him.

"You mean we have to touch them?" Emma S. asked. She frowned. "That's gross!"

"Ooey, gooey, and gross!" George shouted out. But he sounded really happy about it.

Katie laughed. That was George. He loved anything that was disgusting. The more yucky, the better!

"But it's so muddy," Emma S. said.

Katie looked down at the ground. It *was* all wet and muddy. Having kids get mud all over their clothes wasn't something teachers usually did. Of course, Mr. G. wasn't a normal teacher.

The first week of school, Mr. G. made all the kids pretend to be birds and use their mouths as beaks to pick gummy worms out of bowls of chocolate-pudding mud. That had been lots of fun.

"The ground is muddy from the rain last night. You should be able to find lots of earthworms," Mr. G. continued as he handed out small plastic containers to each of the kids.

"What are these for?" Kadeem asked.

"When you find a worm, place it in your container," Mr. G. told him.

Katie took a container and went to work. She wasn't really grossed out by the idea of collecting worms. They were just like any other animals. And Katie loved all animals. Maybe her class was going to study worms in their next learning adventure.

"Oooo. There's a big fat one," Mandy told Katie. She pointed to the ground and made a face. "I can't touch it. Can you get it?"

Katie nodded. She picked up a twig and walked over to the slimy earthworm. She used the stick to push the slimy worm onto a dried leaf. Then she picked up the leaf and dropped the worm into her container.

"That was smart," Emma W. complimented Katie. "I'll try it that way."

Before long, each of the kids had at least one worm in their containers.

"I think I have the most," George said. "I've got three."

"I only have two," Kevin said. "But they're really big ones."

"Shouldn't we collect some leaves and dirt for the worms so they have something to eat when we bring them in the classroom?" Katie asked her teacher.

Mr. G. shook his head. "They're not going to

eat. They're going to be eaten."

Katie gasped. She wasn't sure she had heard her teacher right. "Eaten?" she repeated nervously. Her worms?

Mr. G. nodded. "These worms are a treat for our favorite reptile, Slinky."

"He'll like that," Kevin said happily. "I'm sure he's sick of the pieces of raw fish and crickets he usually gets."

Katie had never liked it that Slinky ate that stuff, but she'd never said anything. Still, this was different. She had found her poor, innocent worms. It would be her fault if they wound up inside Slinky.

"I don't want to feed my worms to Slinky," Katie said. "It's not right to feed one animal to another."

Mr. G. looked at her kindly. "I know how you feel, Katie. But snakes eat worms. That's how nature intended it."

Katie shook her head. "Slinky's not eating my worms," she said. "I wouldn't have collected them if I knew that was what we were doing."

"But . . ." Mr. G. began.

Katie was too upset to listen to her teacher. She poured the earthworms out of her container and watched them squirm back into the mud.

"FREE THE WORMS!" she shouted to her friends.

But the kids didn't hear Katie. They were already following Mr. G. back into the school—with their worms in hand.

Katie sighed. Those poor worms. They didn't realize they would soon be Slinky's lunch!

Chapter 6

"Oh yeah! We've got worms for lunch, too!" George cheered as he sat down at the table and looked at his lunch tray. He picked up his plate and jiggled it so his spaghetti moved around. "Just look at them wiggling around."

"Gross!" Suzanne said.

"Not as gross as what Mr. G. had us doing this morning," Emma S. said. "We were collecting muddy worms."

"That's disgusting," Suzanne said. She looked sympathetically at Emma S. "Too bad you're not in our class. We watched a movie about snakes."

"We get to watch a *real* snake," Kevin

argued. "Slinky. He's going to eat the worms after recess."

Suzanne looked at Katie. "Seriously?" she asked.

Katie sighed. "I don't want to talk about it," she said.

"Katie Kazoo refused to give her worms to Slinky," Emma W. explained to Suzanne. "She set them free."

"I can't kill animals," Katie explained. "Even if it's for Slinky."

"Slinky's gonna love *my* worms," George told the others. "They're really fat and juicy. Snakes have these cool jaws that open really wide. He's going to be able to swallow those fat old worms in one gulp!"

"George, you're making me sick!" Suzanne exclaimed.

George placed a strand of spaghetti in his mouth. "Slinky's gonna slurp the worms up, just like this!" The spaghetti wiggled and jiggled like a real worm as it moved toward his mouth.

"Cut it out, George," Katie said. She blinked a few times, trying not to cry. She felt so bad for the worms in the classroom.

She felt bad about disobeying Mr. G., too.

Basically, she felt bad about everything.

Just then, out of nowhere, Jeremy broke into song. "Lizard on a rock, listening to rock . . ."

"Rock on!" George and Kevin chimed in. "That reptile's goin' wild. Rock on!"

Katie smiled at Jeremy. She knew he had started singing just to change the subject. He wanted her to feel better. What a good friend!

"Hey, have you guys thought about a name for our band yet?" Jeremy asked George and Kevin. "I was thinking we could be called the Rhythm Rockers. After all, we're going to have a really good rhythm coming from my drums."

Kevin made a face.

"I think we should call ourselves George and the Jokers," George suggested.

"Why should *your* name be part of the *band's* name?" Jeremy asked.

"Because I came up with the idea for the band in the first place," George said.

"Yeah, but I'm the one who talked to Mr. Starkey," Kevin reminded him. "That's why he's letting us use the band room for practice. And I got him to promise to help us with our music, too."

Katie had once heard Mr. Starkey play the drums with his rock band, the Downhill Slide. He was a very talented musician. If Mr. Starkey was helping the guys, they might really become a great band one day.

If only they could stop arguing.

Katie really hated it when her friends fought. So she tried to tune out the argument and focus on her food. But after what George had said, the spaghetti just looked like a plate of tomato-covered worms.

This day was turning out so awful. The only good thing was that poem she'd written about Slinky.

The poem! Katie had almost forgotten that she'd wanted to draw a picture of Slinky to go with it. Maybe Mr. G. would let her do that during recess.

"Where are you going?" Suzanne asked as Katie got up from the table.

"Back to our classroom," she told her. "There's something I have to do."

"You'd rather spend recess in the classroom than out on the playground with us?" George asked her.

Katie nodded.

"Why?" Jeremy wondered.

"Slinky can't talk," she told them as she walked away. "Which means he can't argue, either."

Chapter 7

"Thanks for letting me stay here during recess, Mr. G.," Katie told her teacher a few minutes later.

"No problem," Mr. G. told her. "I think it's great that you want to draw Slinky."

"And I wasn't doodling in class like I used to," Katie reminded him. She wanted to make sure that Mr. G. knew that she usually tried to do what her teacher told her to. "I waited until recess to draw."

Mr. G. grinned. "I noticed," he told her. "Good job."

Katie sat down on the floor near Slinky's cage. She pulled a pencil from her backpack and began to sketch the snake.

It wasn't easy. Slinky's face was partially hidden by a big wooden tree branch in his cage. Katie wished he would wiggle somewhere else, so she could get a better view. But the snake was just lying there. And it didn't look like he was going anywhere anytime soon.

"I've got to make some copies of a story in the office," Mr. G. told Katie. "You can stay here and work."

"Okay," Katie told him.

"If you finish before I get back, just pack away your notebook and markers and go out to the playground," Mr. G. continued.

Katie nodded and went back to drawing. But after a few minutes, she stopped. Her drawing wasn't all that great. The problem was, she couldn't really see Slinky's face because it was blocked by the branch.

Katie tapped on the side of the glass cage, hoping Slinky would wake up and move. But it didn't work. The snake just lay there.

Katie sighed. If only she could take Slinky out of his cage to get a good look at him.

Deep down, Katie knew Mr. G. probably wouldn't want her to do that. But it would just be for a few minutes. She'd have Slinky back in his cage before Mr. G. returned from the copy machine.

Quickly, Katie removed the wire top from Slinky's cage. She reached in and gently lifted the small black, yellow, red, and white snake from the floor of his cage.

Slinky's body stiffened slightly at Katie's touch. She petted him gently as she placed him on her beanbag chair.

"It's okay," she told Slinky in a soothing voice. "I just want to draw you. I would never hurt you."

Just then, Katie felt a cool breeze on the back of her neck. She gulped. Cold air wouldn't be good for Slinky. He was a cold-blooded animal. His temperature changed to match the temperature around him. That was why there was a heater in his tank. Slinky had to be kept warm. A cool, breezy room was no place for a snake.

Katie would have to put Slinky back and figure out a different way to draw him up close. But before Katie could even pick up the snake, the gentle breeze grew stronger.

A lot stronger. In fact, it was a wild, whirling tornado!

A tornado that was spinning only around Katie!

Katie gulped. Oh no! This wasn't any ordinary wind. This was the magic wind. It was back!

The magic wind whirled faster and faster. It was so powerful that Katie thought she might be blown right out of the classroom.

Then, an even worse thought flashed in her mind. Slinky was so tiny and helpless. What if the wind blew him away, too? He'd never be able to find his way back.

But there was nothing Katie could do

about that. The magic wind wasn't something she could control. She shut her eyes tight and tried not to cry.

Then, suddenly, it stopped. Just like that. The magic wind was gone.

And so was Katie Kazoo.

She'd turned into someone else . . . one, two, switcheroo.

But who?

Chapter 8

Slowly, Katie turned her head. Oh no! The really cool red sneakers she had worn to school that morning were gone.

In fact, her *feet* were gone! So were her legs and her arms. Not to mention her hands, fingers, eyelids, and ears.

Katie couldn't hear a thing. But she could smell. And from where she was lying, she could sense the faint scent of food. She wasn't sure what kind of food, though. Katie stuck out her long, forked tongue to get a better whiff.

Her *tongue*? Katie gasped. How could she be smelling with her tongue?

Just then, Katie remembered something

Mr. G. had taught the class earlier in the week. There was one kind of reptile that smelled using sensors in its tongue . . . a snake!

That's when it hit her. The magic wind had switcherooed Katie into a snake. And not just any snake. *Slinky* the snake!

At the moment, Slinky was one hungry snake. His stomach was grumbling. Or at least Katie *thought* it was Slinky's stomach she felt grumbling. It was hard to tell where Slinky's stomach might be in his long, narrow snake body.

Wherever it was, it was empty. Now Katie wished she'd eaten some of that spaghetti at lunch. Too bad the food had reminded her of worms.

Although . . . come to think of it . . . right now a wriggly worm seemed tasty. Even though her Katie mind still thought it was wrong to eat animals, her snake senses were actually craving the worms. Kevin was right. Worms were definitely something Slinky would consider a treat.

But no matter how good those worms might taste right now, there was no way Katie could get to them. The worm containers were up on a high shelf. It would take a lot of wiggling for her to get up there.

Katie didn't have nearly enough strength to try that. She was so tired. She didn't feel like doing anything but sleeping. Yes! That sounded so nice. If she were home right now she would just crawl under the covers, shut her eyes, and take a nice nap.

But Katie wasn't home right now. So if she was going to fall asleep, it would have to be right here, in the middle of a cozy beanbag chair.

Aaaaahhhh. Katie opened her mouth wide and tried to yawn. Ooh. That felt awful. Like her skin was too tight or something. And she felt like she really needed to scratch.

If she were a fourth-grade girl again, she could have used a fingernail. But right now she didn't have fingers, never mind finger*nails*. If only she were still in her cage—well, *Slinky's* cage, actually—she'd be able to scratch her body on that wooden tree branch.

She looked around the room. The legs of the table that held Slinky's cage were wooden. Quickly she began wriggling her body, forcing herself to move toward the table.

The table seemed miles and miles away. But she was feeling more and more uncomfortable in her tight snakeskin. Katie just had to get to that wooden table leg.

So on she slithered.

And jiggled.

And turned.

And squirmed. Until, finally, she reached the table leg.

Yahoo! Katie thought to herself. I made it!

Katie placed her snake mouth against the wooden leg and moved her head up and down. *Scratch. Scratch. Scratch.*

Aaaahhh. Katie let out a hiss-like sigh. That felt much better. The itching around her mouth

was practically gone now.

Unfortunately, the tight, itching feeling was moving down her body. Katie scrunched forward a little bit, so she could scratch lower down.

That's when she realized something. Her head felt different than the rest of her body. It was freer, and more comfortable. Like it was new skin.

New skin. She knew what that meant.

Slinky was shedding!

Which meant *Katie* was shedding.

Katie opened her mouth and hissed in fear. It wasn't as good as a cry, but it was all she could do right now.

Then she got back to business. Katie just had to get out of that tight snakeskin!

Scratch. Scratch. Scratch.

Chapter 9

Hooray!

With one last scratch of her tail against the wood, Slinky's old skin was completely cut open. Katie crawled out of it and slithered around joyfully. The new skin fit perfectly on her snake body.

Clomp. Clomp. Clomp. Clomp.

Just then, Katie felt strong vibrations coming from the hall. She couldn't hear the sounds, but somehow she knew what was happening. Those were footsteps. They were heading in her direction. Someone was on his way to Class 4A.

Oh no! It had to be Mr. G.! He was on his way back from the copy machine.

Clomp. Clomp.

He was getting really close now. Any second he'd be in the room.

When he got there, Mr. G. would see Katie's markers and her notebook on the floor. He would be upset that she had not cleaned up her mess.

But that was nothing compared to how angry Mr. G. would be to find Slinky on the floor instead of in his cage. When the magic wind came and changed Katie back into herself, she was definitely going to be in big trouble.

That is, *if* the magic wind ever came back. It seemed to Katie that the wind had left her in Slinky's body an awfully long time. Long enough for her to shed her skin completely, anyway.

What if this was the one time the magic wind decided to go away for good? Katie would have to spend the rest of her life shedding her skin and waiting for the kids in class 4A to feed her fish, crickets, and the occasional worm.

Hisss . . . Hisss . . . Katie let out the saddest snake sound ever heard.

Clomp. Clomp. Clomp. Clomp.

The vibrations in the hall were getting stronger and stronger. Which meant Mr. G. was getting closer and closer. Katie's little snake heart began to pound wildly.

Then . . . suddenly . . . the footsteps stopped. Just like that.

Phew! Mr. G. must have bumped into another teacher in the hall or something, Katie thought to herself. *They're probably out there right now talking about teacher stuff.*

At just that moment, Katie felt a cool breeze blowing on the back of her head. Almost instantly, her whole snake body grew cold— just like the breeze.

Katie began wiggling back over to the beanbag chair, hoping to curl up inside and warm up. But before she could squirm more than a few inches, the wind picked up speed, blowing harder and harder. In a second it became a powerful tornado that was blowing just around Katie.

The magic wind was back. And as scary as that wild wind felt, Katie was glad it had arrived. Once she was back in her own skin, she'd get Slinky back in his cage before Mr. G. returned to the classroom.

Katie braced her snake body against the magic wind. She didn't have to try not to cry— she knew she couldn't. There was nothing she could do but wait for the tornado to be over.

And in a few seconds, it was. The magic wind was gone.

And Katie Kazoo was back!

The first thing she did was wiggle all of her fingers and toes.

She sniffed the air—with her nose.

"Oh yeah!" Katie cheered. She shook her arms and legs and did a happy dance. It was so nice not to be a snake anymore.

Then Katie heard footsteps in the hallway. Mr. G.!

"Come on, Slinky," Katie said. "It's time to go home to your cage."

When Katie looked down at the ground, she didn't see Slinky. He was gone!

Quickly, Katie got down on her hands and knees and started looking around the corners of the room for Slinky. It was as if he'd just disappeared by magic.

Magic! Oh no! Had the magic wind blown him away?

It must have. There was no other explanation.

Which meant Slinky could be just about anywhere in the whole world. That magic wind was really strong.

Poor Slinky. He was in a new place, all by himself. He was probably really scared. And even hungrier.

Katie was scared, too. How was she ever going to explain this to Mr. G.—or to the other kids in her class? It was all her fault that Slinky had disappeared. They were going to be mad at her forever!

This was s-s-sooo not good!

Chapter 10

"Hi, Katie," Mr. G. said as he walked into the classroom. "Almost finished with your drawing?"

Katie frowned. She was finished, all right.

Mr. G. looked at her curiously. "What's wrong?"

"It's Slinky, he . . . uh . . ." Katie stammered nervously. "W–w–well, I was drawing him, but his face was hidden by that branch. I wanted to get a better look so I . . ."

"So you took him out of his cage," Mr. G. said, finishing her sentence. "Katie, you're not supposed to do that."

"I know," Katie said sadly. "I'm really sorry."

"We'll talk about it later," Mr. G. told her, sounding a little angry and disappointed. "Right now, I want you to put Slinky back in his cage." He looked around the room. "Where is he?"

Uh-oh! Now Mr. G. was going to be really mad!

"Th-that's just it," Katie stammered. "I don't know. I've been looking all over for him."

"What do you mean?" Mr. G. asked her.

"Well, after I took him out of his cage, he kind of slithered over to that table leg," Katie told her teacher. "He started rubbing his body on the wood. And then his skin popped open and he crawled out."

"Slinky was shedding right before your eyes," Mr. G. said. "That must have been very interesting to see."

"It was really tight and itchy," Katie said.

Oops. There was no way a fourth-grade girl could know something like that.

"I mean, um . . . er . . . he looked like he was very itchy. After that, I only turned away for a few seconds. Honest," Katie continued, tears welling in her eyes. "But when I looked down again, he was gone. Now he's probably far away, scared and all alone."

"Snakes aren't all that fast," Mr. G. assured her. "He's around here somewhere. A snake couldn't just disappear."

Yes, he could, Katie thought to herself. But

she really wanted to believe Mr. G. was right.

"There has to be a way to coax Slinky out of hiding," Mr. G. continued, thinking out loud. "We just have to figure out what it is."

Katie sighed. This wasn't going to be easy. After all, Slinky wasn't going to come running at the sound of his name like Pepper did. For one thing, Slinky couldn't hear. And for another, he didn't have any legs to run on.

Then, suddenly, Katie got one of her great ideas! "Slinky's very hungry," she told Mr. G.

Her teacher looked at her curiously.

"I mean, he must be," Katie corrected herself quickly. "We haven't fed him yet. And it takes a lot of energy to shed your skin. What with all that scratching and wriggling and all."

"True," Mr. G. said.

"I bet he'd come out for a worm," Katie suggested.

Mr. G. shot Katie a curious look. "I thought you didn't think we should feed the worms to Slinky," he said.

Katie nodded. "That's what I used to think. But now I understand that Slinky has to eat the kind of food that will keep him healthy. He's not like humans. We can choose from all sorts of foods and still stay healthy."

Mr. G. smiled. "Exactly."

"But I don't want to be the one to feed Slinky the worm," Katie admitted. "I just couldn't do that."

Mr. G. nodded understandingly. "I'll feed it to him. As soon as we find him," he added as he went up on the shelf and grabbed one of the containers of worms.

Mr. G. opened the lid of the container to let the scent of the worms into the air.

Katie imagined Slinky sticking out his long, forked tongue to get a good whiff.

Katie stood there beside her teacher, waiting for Slinky to slither out.

She waited.

And waited.

And waited.

But nothing happened.

"This is all my fault," Katie cried out. "Slinky is gone forever!"

Mr. G. shook his head and grinned. "Not exactly," he said. "Look over there."

Katie looked in the direction Mr. G. was pointing. At first she didn't see anything. But then she noticed something funny. Kadeem's backpack was lying open on the floor. And it was moving.

"He's in there!" Katie shouted out excitedly. "He's in the backpack!"

"Putting out the worms was a great suggestion, Katie," Mr. G. said. "He must have picked up their scent."

"With his tongue," Katie added.

"Exactly," Mr. G. agreed. He bent down and gently pulled Slinky from Kadeem's backpack. "Now let's get this guy back in his cage and feed him."

Katie turned her back when Mr. G. put a worm in Slinky's cage. She looked down at the floor and tried not to picture Slinky swallowing his prey.

A few minutes later, Katie watched as her teacher pinned Slinky's shed skin onto the bulletin board.

"Our little guy is growing up," Mr. G. joked. "He's gone up a size."

Katie giggled, picturing Slinky in a T-shirt and jeans—the kinds of things she and her mother went shopping for when Katie grew to a new size.

"Snakes are definitely lucky," Katie told her teacher.

"Why?" Mr. G. asked.

"They don't have to wait on line at a store to try things on," she answered with a laugh. "And their new skin is always a perfect fit."

Chapter 11

"Hey, Katie, where have you been?" Suzanne asked at the end of the school day. "I've been waiting outside the school for you for*ever!*"

Katie laughed. Actually, it had only been fifteen minutes since the bell had rung. As usual, Suzanne was exaggerating.

"I was cleaning Slinky's cage," she told Suzanne.

Suzanne made a face. "Why would you want to do that?"

"Because he deserves it," Katie replied. "He had a tough day."

"How tough can a snake's day be?" Suzanne asked her.

"Slinky shed his skin today," Katie explained. "You have no idea how exhausting that can be."

"And you do?" Suzanne chuckled.

Katie didn't answer. What could she say?

"Well, anyway, you missed everything," Suzanne went on.

"What's everything?" Katie asked.

Suzanne grinned. She really loved being the person who was in the know. "Well, for starters, the band broke up."

"Broke up?" Katie repeated. "But they just got together."

Suzanne shrugged. "And now they're apart."

"Was this all over that name thing?" Katie wondered.

Suzanne nodded. "Fourth-grade boys are such babies."

Katie sighed. "I sure wish I could help get the band back together."

"Well, you can't," Suzanne told her.

Katie looked at her strangely. Suzanne seemed almost happy about that.

"At least we still have the Bayside Boys," Suzanne said. "They'll always be our favorite group."

"I wonder how they got *their* name," Katie said.

"Oh, I know that. I read all about it on their website," Suzanne boasted. "They all grew up as boys in San Francisco. That's a city located on a bay. So they're the Bayside Boys."

"That makes sense," Katie said.

"It's a good name," Suzanne told her. "It really catches your attention."

Katie sure wished she could help the boys come up with a name like that. Maybe she could have helped them to keep their band together.

But Slinky had needed her, too.

Slinky!

Suddenly Katie had another one of her great ideas.

"Do you want to go to my house and look at the Bayside Boys website?" Suzanne asked Katie.

Katie shook her head. "I can't," she told her. "I have something really important to do at home."

"More important than the Bayside Boys?" Suzanne asked.

Katie nodded. "Believe it or not, yes," she said.

✕ ✕ ✕

When Katie arrived at school the next morning, there was a lot of tension on the playground. George was standing all by himself near the big tree glaring at Kevin. Jeremy was sitting on the bench, glaring at George. And Kevin was over by the swings glaring at Jeremy and George.

Katie walked over to Jeremy first. "I have a surprise for you guys," she told him.

"What guys?" Jeremy asked her.

"You and George and Kevin. The band," Katie said.

"There is no band," Jeremy told her. "We broke up."

"Oh yeah, Suzanne mentioned that," Katie admitted. "But I didn't believe her."

"Well, you should have," Jeremy said.

Katie didn't answer. Instead she took Jeremy by the hand and pulled him over to where George was standing. "Hi, George," she said.

"Hi, Katie," George replied. He ignored Jeremy.

"I have a surprise for the band," Katie said.

"There is no band," George and Jeremy said at once.

"Nice harmony," Katie told them. "That will come in handy when you're singing."

George and Jeremy scowled at each other. But Katie paid no attention.

"Kevin!" she called across the playground. "Come here."

Kevin didn't move. He obviously didn't want to be near George and Jeremy.

Katie took both Jeremy and George by the hands and pulled them across the blacktop.

"Stop it, Katie," Jeremy said.

"I don't want to talk to them," George insisted.

But Katie didn't stop until she reached where Kevin was standing.

"Hi, Katie," Kevin said, ignoring George and Jeremy.

"Hi," Katie replied. "I have a surprise for the three of you."

The boys all watched as Katie reached into her backpack. "Here it is," she told them as she pulled out three T-shirts. "Tada!"

"Wow!" Jeremy exclaimed.

"Those are so cool!" Kevin added.

"Amazing," George agreed.

Katie grinned. She knew the T-shirts were awesome. She'd spent all yesterday afternoon decorating them in red, white, yellow, and black. And she'd taken a really long time writing the new band name she'd come up with on the front.

"Slinky and the Worms," Jeremy read. "I like that."

"Yeah, it's funny," George agreed.

"No one will forget it," Kevin added.

"So now you guys can be a band again," Katie told the boys.

This time the boys didn't argue with her.

"We'll wear these at every gig we play," Jeremy promised her.

"Definitely," George and Kevin agreed.

Katie grinned. The band was back together.

"There's just one thing," Kevin pointed out.

"What?" George asked him.

"Which one of us is Slinky?" Kevin wondered. "I mean, I'd much rather be a snake than a worm."

"Yeah, well, so would I," Jeremy said.

"Slinky's not even your class pet," George told Jeremy. "You guys have a guinea pig."

"So what?" Jeremy asked. "I still think Slinky's cool."

"*I* think he's cooler," George told him.

Oh, no. It was starting all over again. Katie had to do something, and fast!

"Why don't you guys take turns being Slinky?" Katie suggested.

"Yeah, we could do that," Jeremy said.

"Sure," Kevin agreed.

George slipped on his T-shirt. "Katie Kazoo," he said. "You know what?"

"What?" Katie asked him.

"You rock!" George exclaimed.

Katie grinned. "Rock on, dudes," she said.

"Rock on!" Kevin, George, and Jeremy answered all at once. "Rock on!"

Surprising Snake Facts!

1. There are 2,267 known species of snakes in the world today.
2. Snakes are deaf, but they do feel vibrations in the ground they are resting on. (Surprise! That means a cobra can't really hear a snake charmer's flute. The snake moves because of the vibrations the music makes.)
3. Snakes can open their jaws so wide that they are able to swallow prey that is bigger than their heads.

4. The smallest snakes are Brahminy blind snakes. They only grow to about two inches long.

5. The largest snake, the anaconda, can grow as long as thirty-eight feet.

About the Author

NANCY KRULIK is the author of more than 150 books for children and young adults, including three *New York Times* bestsellers. She lives in New York City with her husband, composer Daniel Burwasser, their children, Amanda and Ian, and Pepper, a chocolate and white spaniel mix. When she's not busy writing the *Katie Kazoo, Switcheroo* series, Nancy loves swimming, reading, and going to the movies.

About the Illustrators

JOHN & WENDY'S art has been featured in other books for children, in magazines, on stationery, and on toys. When they are not drawing Katie and her friends, they like to paint, take photographs, travel, and play music in their rock 'n' roll band. They live and work in Brooklyn, New York.

How to
Pass that
Job
Interview

Visit our How To website at www.howto.co.uk

At **www.howto.co.uk** you can engage in conversation with our authors – all of whom have 'been there and done that' in their specialist fields. You can get access to special offers and additional content but most importantly you will be able to engage with, and become a part of, a wide and growing community of people just like yourself.

At **www.howto.co.uk** you'll be able to talk and share tips with people who have similar interests and are facing similar challenges in their lives. People who, just like you, have the desire to change their lives for the better – be it through moving to a new country, starting a new business, growing your own vegetables, or writing a novel.

At **www.howto.co.uk** you'll find the support and encouragement you need to help make your aspirations a reality.

You can go direct to **www.how-to-pass-that-job-interview.co.uk** which is part of the main How To site.

How To Books strives to present authentic, inspiring, practical information in their books. Now, when you buy a title from **How To Books**, you get even more than just words on a page.

How to Pass that Job Interview

Julie-Ann Amos

howtobooks

Published by How To Books Ltd,
Spring Hill House, Spring Hill Road, Begbroke,
Oxford OX5 1RX. United Kingdom.
Tel: (01865) 375794. Fax: (01865) 379162
info@howtobooks.co.uk
www.howtobooks.co.uk

How To Books greatly reduce the carbon footprint of their books
by sourcing their typesetting and printing in the UK.

First edition 2002
Second edition 2004
Third edition 2008
Reprinted 2008
Fourth edition 2009
Fifth edition 2010

British Library Cataloguing in Publication Data.
A catalogue record for this book is available from the British Library.

978 1 84528 426 8

Produced for How To Books by Deer Park Productions, Tavistock
Typeset by Kestrel Data, Exeter
Cover design by Baseline Arts Ltd, Oxford
Printed and bound in Great Britain by Bell & Bain Ltd, Glasgow

NOTE: The material contained in this book is set out in good faith for general
guidance and no liability can be accepted for loss or expense incurred as a
result of relying in particular circumstances on statements made in this book.
Laws and regulations are complex and liable to change, and readers should
check the current position with the relevant authorities before making
personal arrangements.

*We have attempted to acknowledge all known sources. We apologise for any that have
been missed. Please contact us so that we can include an acknowledgement in the next
edition.*

10.20   650.144
         Amo

Contents

Preface

Job interviews can be daunting. This book will take you through the essentials of preparing for a successful interview. Whether it is your first interview, or your first in a long time – or even if you are an 'old hand' – you will find tips and hints for success.

Interviews can be some of the most stressful situations we have to face. From the moment you enter the potential employer's building to the time you are back outside, you are on show – and preparing to give a good performance is what can guarantee success. You *can* tip the scales in your favour, with a little work beforehand.

Julie-Ann Amos

Chapter 1

Preparing for Interviews

Preparing for interviews starts before you even know you have an interview.

In this Chapter:

♦ **the purpose of interviews**
♦ **preparation**
♦ **getting your paperwork in order**
♦ **researching the company**
♦ **researching yourself**
♦ **getting from your front door to the interview.**

You can start your preparation before you even know you've been invited to an interview. Understanding the purpose of interviews, and being aware of the contents of your own curriculum vitae or application form is the first step of essential preparation for any interview.

You will need to assemble your job application paperwork carefully and put it in order so you can respond to short-notice invitations to attend interviews. Job hunting isn't easy and you may be surprised at the amount of organisation it takes.

For example, you may need to assemble facts and figures about your salary history and financial requirements, etc. Once invited to an interview, you will also need to assemble some information on the company that's interviewing you, but of course there's no point in preparing detailed information on companies until you know you've got an interview with them.

Is this you?

♦ Surely you can't prepare much for interviews, apart from getting basic information on the company that's going to interview you?

♦ Look, I know who I am and what jobs I've done. I don't need to memorise my own CV – I was there!

♦ I spend ages preparing and getting organised, but it's all wasted when I don't get an interview.

♦ I've sent off so many job applications that I can't remember who's who. It's all a bit of a mess, really.

The purpose of interviews

There's more than one type of interview – nowadays, interviews take many different forms (as we shall see) so that being aware of the different types of interview you may encounter can be very helpful. The How To book *Handling Tough Job Interviews*, also by Julie-Ann Amos, is very helpful in this regard but here are some of the main types.

Recruitment agency interviews

Recruitment agencies exist to place people in jobs. They make their money from the employer – the recruiter – and not from you. Therefore, the common assumption that recruitment agencies are there to help you may be a slight misconception.

Good agencies can be extremely helpful in looking after job hunters properly, by giving them help and support, and placing them in the right job. Others are purely serving the employment needs of the companies and organisations that pay their fees. They may be less concerned with meeting your own individual wants and needs, and more concerned with placing you in a job – any job – that will earn them a fee.

So recruitment agency interviews can be beneficial, as they will give you an opportunity to check out the agency and the way it operates. In an ideal world, the recruitment agency interview should be no more than a means of letting your agency know exactly what you want in a job – so it can tailor any applications it makes on your behalf specifically to your needs. Be aware of the way some agencies operate, however, and watch out for any attempt to 'sell you' a job that isn't in line with your requirements.

With a good agency, an interview can give you tips and advice on presenting yourself well, information on your strong and weaker points, and advice on how to conduct yourself in interviews with potential employers.

Employer interviews

Employer interviews are designed to allow the employer to assess whether or not you are a good fit with their requirements. Usually, a first interview is very much a screening interview, with a second interview being held later for those candidates who pass this initial screening. Your performance at the first interview should therefore really be a matter of being seen to be right for the job. Later interviews are where you would prove yourself to be the *best* candidate.

Personnel or Human Resources (HR) interviews

You will often encounter personnel or HR interviews, as most larger companies insist on them as part of the recruitment process. These interviews are sometimes viewed as 'easy', as HR interviewers rarely ask very technical questions about your specific skills – as they are HR specialists and not usually business managers. Questions are far more likely to revolve around other, more personal areas. But these interviews are not to be underestimated – HR specialists are often very highly trained and experienced in interviewing, and they usually carry out interviews on a regular basis. They are therefore skilled at getting information from you, so be careful – never attempt to pull the wool over their eyes.

> Not all interviews are alike – be aware of the purpose of an interview, and this will help you do well in all circumstances.

Preparation

Getting prepared is really what the whole of this book is about. So what exactly is it that you have to prepare? The first two chapters of the book focus on things you can *do* before the interview, and the rest of the book details information you can consider and think over before the interview as a means of preparing yourself for it.

Here are some examples of what you should prepare, ready for a round of potential interviews.

Paperwork
This includes your CV, a copy of the relevant application form, and all documents relating to a particular interview. Have copies of everything to hand well in advance – don't rely on technology (which can let you down) to print copies for you at the last minute.

Your 'shopping list'
Too many people attend interviews with no clear idea of exactly what they want and need from them. Make

sure you know what you do and don't want in terms of salary, environment, benefits, role etc.

Research

Make sure you have ready access to any research about the job, the company or organisation you have undertaken previously (see later). It may help you ask questions at interview or help you identify areas you need to clarify to see if this job opportunity meets your wants and needs list – your 'shopping list'.

What you will wear and take

All too often people leave these decisions until the last moment, rushing round looking for the right outfit on interview day. If you can, have your interview outfit cleaned in advance and ready to wear at short notice.

Transport

You need to research and plan the means of transport you intend to use to get to and from the interview. Thinking ahead will allow you to avoid running the risk of being late.

Things to think about

In addition, you will need to think about:

♦ how you will introduce yourself

♦ how to stay calm and relaxed, in what is for most people a stressful situation

♦ how to deal with the interviewer's questions

♦ preparing some sample answers to likely questions

- ◆ your body language, and how to establish a good rapport with your interviewer

- ◆ how to leave the interview gracefully and on a good note.

There are two stages to preparation – physically preparing, and mentally/academically thinking through the interview and potential difficulties you may encounter when you are interviewed.

Getting your paperwork in order

You need to make and have to hand copies of all your essential paperwork relating to the interviewer. You will need a copy of your CV, a copy of any job applications you send off, and the job adverts you are responding to. Of course, all this paperwork can be daunting and expensive to photocopy if you don't have access to a copier – and it can be hard to manage.

Be organised

Consider some sort of filing system. A cheap solution is a simple file or ring binder, in which you can collate job adverts and information by filing them, cutting out job adverts and sticking them onto A4 sheets of paper as necessary. This is important – if you get an interview, you need to be able to read what you have available on the job and the company, and you need to check **exactly** what the employer is looking for, so you can tailor your thinking and preparation to giving a good performance for a particular job interview.

The filing system you use isn't important – what is important is that if anyone calls you to arrange an interview, you can find the information you need easily so you can prepare properly. You don't want to be getting stressed and anxious looking for the job advert in a pile of papers – you need to be calm and to prepare your thoughts carefully if you want to do well at the interview.

Job adverts

Job adverts usually give you a good idea of the skills and abilities the employer is looking for, so you need to read the job advert carefully if you are to prepare properly for an interview. If you are applying for a lot of jobs from adverts, you will need to be very organised, and to keep copies of all the adverts you reply to.

Application forms or packs

You will also need to consider application forms. If you have applied for jobs which involve filling out application forms, ideally you should keep a copy of the form you complete. You don't need to keep a copy of your basic details such as education, job history etc, as this is information that will be on your CV. But you do need to keep a copy of your answers to questions on the form such as 'Describe how you fit the job description', or 'Outline why you feel you are right for this role'. Your responses to questions like these may well be discussed at interview, so you really need to read through what you said on the form before going to the interview.

It's very useful that when an application form is sent to you, it will usually be part of a 'candidate pack', that will give you information such as a job description, structure of the company department, etc. This is all good stuff that will help you to prepare for your interview. Again, it needs to be filed so you can find it when you need it – there's no worse way of preparing for an interview than having to conduct a last-minute paper chase!

You have a lot of resources available to help you prepare for interviews, but keeping them all organised and easily to hand can be almost as stressful as the interview itself!

Researching the company

Application or candidate packs
As mentioned above, when you get an application form, it will often be part of an application pack or candidate pack produced by the organisation. These packs can sometimes be very scrappy and hastily put together, but many of them are very well-presented and give you incredibly useful information about:

♦ what exactly the employer is looking for

♦ whether the employer's requirements are essential or desirable

- ♦ how the employer will test whether or not you fit a particular requirement

- ♦ special skills and abilities required by the employer

- ♦ information on working conditions at the workplace

- ♦ information about the organisation

- ♦ organisation charts setting out company/ departmental structures

- ♦ background to the department and/or the job

- ♦ details of salary and benefits, etc

- ♦ the recruitment process, and timescales relating to the process.

These packs can be the single most useful thing you have available to you for interview preparation, so keep them safe and read them carefully before the interview. They can help you understand how to present yourself in the best possible light, and give you ideas for questions to raise and points to clarify with the interviewer. Most importantly, they can give you a real feel for the job and the company they describe, which can be very useful in helping you decide whether or not the job is really for you.

If the company doesn't send you a pack, be proactive – call them and ask them for one. If you are invited to an interview, ask them to send you any information on the company they may have. Often companies send out a letter confirming an interview, and/or directions, so when they do, ask them to send you their company literature. If you don't ask, you don't get!

Other sources of company information

Even if you aren't sent an application pack, you can still obtain useful and relevant company information prior to your interview. You can research companies through media such as the internet, reference libraries and papers/journals, for example. Look for any material that will lead to increasing your knowledge of the company.

It is absolutely crucial you understand the culture and environment of the company by whom you will be interviewed, so that you can make the right decision as to whether you would be happy working for them. Research the organisation's history, its current market situation, clients, competitors etc.

The company website

Websites can give you a wealth of information about companies. If you don't know the address of a company's website, look it up by using one of the major research engines such as Yahoo! or Google.

Other internet websites

Here are some other good internet website sources of business information (correct at the time of printing).

www.prnewswire.co.uk
This is a European news network that covers press

releases and features. Allows searching for press releases by company name.

http://news.bbc.co.uk/hi/english/business/companies
This is the BBC news service that will give you all the latest news on companies.

www.thetimes.co.uk
You need to register to use this, but registration is currently free. There are selected news stories, from the latest editions of the two papers. You can search the archive back to January '96.

www.digitallook.com/dlmedia/news/company_news?
Another site with live company news feed, but not easy to search as for example the BBC website.

Libraries
The reference section of your local library may have useful business directories such as Kompass, Dunn & Bradstreet and Kellys.

Papers/journals
Trade magazines are another useful source of company information.

Application packs are fantastic resources for interview preparation. Always ask for application packs where possible.

Researching yourself

Is this the job you really want?

As you have just read, application packs can help you decide whether or not a job is right for you. An essential part of your interview preparation should always be to evaluate your own needs, wants and desires. If you assess carefully how badly you want this particular job, you will approach the interview with the right mindset.

If you don't really feel the job is ideal for you, but that it's one you could settle for, you can approach the interview more as a means for giving you interview experience. But if the job is the one you really want – that elusive 'dream job' – then the interview becomes extremely important, and you will need to put all your effort into excelling at it.

Know your facts

You may be asked in detail at interview about your salary and benefits expectations. Make sure you know what these are, as you may look rather foolish if you don't. Check out your hourly, weekly or monthly rate (however you are paid) and when you last had a pay rise. Know what benefits you get. If you don't know what you're paid at the moment, you will weaken your negotiating power.

Know what you want

Look at the job, and before you go into the interview decide the minimum salary or pay you would accept, should you be offered it. The job advert may list a salary or salary range, but a company may sometimes pay more for the right person, so always do your homework and decide on your minimum requirements.

When deciding your minimum requirements, you need to factor in additional costs. For example, if you will have a longer journey, your travelling expenses may be higher than you currently pay. Factor in extra costs like this to your requirements, so you can define:

♦ your ideal salary

♦ your minimum acceptable salary – your 'bottom line'.

It is absolutely essential that you know your absolute bottom line, so if you are offered a salary below this, you will know you need to decline the job offer.

Research salary requirements

Employers are very often open to a well-argued justification for a salary offer. If you have done your homework, and are able to show this by justifying your salary requirements, they are much more likely to be met.

You can do this by looking at other adverts for similar jobs, or talking to people you know in similar jobs, etc. People who can produce evidence that they have researched their requirements are far more likely to get them accepted.

Take some credentials

Don't go overboard, but if it is appropriate take
to the interview some work you have done – drawings
you have done, or papers, reports you have written,
etc.

> Research how badly you want the job, your
> current position and needs, and your salary
> requirements. Knowing the facts and doing the
> necessary research will almost always pay
> dividends.

Getting from your front door to the interview

One area you need to prepare in advance is how you
will actually get to the interview. You need to check
out, well in advance, both *how* you will get there –
bus, taxi, car, train – and *how long* this is likely to take.

Be on time

Being late for interviews isn't necessarily the end of
the world – a pleasant apology and good excuse can
prevent problems – but if an interviewer is working to
a schedule, you may end up not being able to have a
proper interview. Candidates turning up 30 minutes
late for a 45-minute interview place the interviewer in
a dilemma – do they give you a 30-minute interview
and 'steal' 15 minutes from their next candidate? That
isn't fair! Or do they only give you 15 minutes, which
more or less means you won't stand a chance! Don't
put them in that position – be on time.

Check schedules

Don't just plan to get a bus or train – actually check the departure and arrival times. Changes in schedule, repairs, etc can all stop scheduled services from running to plan. Check for last-minute updates, by using facilities such as train websites, AA Roadwatch on teletext, etc.

Be prepared for an emergency

Take a mobile phone, or change for the telephone with you – that way you can call ahead in an emergency, or if you are delayed.

Be generous

Be generous with your time. Delays, breakdowns, traffic, missed trains/buses, etc – all are reasonable, but at the same time avoidable excuses for being late. Allow sufficient time to get to the interview early, then find somewhere nearby to wait in comfort, so you can relax. Nothing makes people more stressed than a rushed journey, getting to the interview late or with seconds to spare. Plan to get there early and wait around – you can always use the time to prepare for your interview further, read through any notes, etc.

Plan your journey carefully, and allow extra time for unforeseen circumstances. Emergencies may be understandable, but getting there late can still mean you don't get a proper interview.

Summary points

♦ Understand the purpose of interviews, so you can structure your preparation accordingly.

♦ Prepare all the necessary information – if you don't need to use it, at least you had it ready.

♦ Get all your paperwork ready – organise it so you can easily find the information you need.

♦ Research the company interviewing you so you can ask them sensible questions and resolve any queries you may have.

♦ Research your own wants and needs – and be prepared to justify them if necessary.

♦ Plan your journey with military precision, so everything goes smoothly on the day.

Chapter 2

Presentation

Presentation is your window-dressing — the shop front you display to the world. A good display attracts more customers and makes them more likely to buy!

In this Chapter:

♦ **making a good impression**
♦ **what to wear**
♦ **personal presentation**
♦ **waiting.**

The best candidate can let themselves down and even lose a job at interview by being poorly presented. We all know it's wrong to judge by appearances, but let's face it, you also have to take human nature into account – people do. Before interviewing you, an interviewer will have made themselves look presentable, arranged a room, refreshments, read your CV, and prepared questions to ask you. In return, it is perfectly natural (and not unreasonable) for them to expect you to have made some effort yourself.

Presentation is all about appearances. A poor candidate can look good and make a decent impression by looking as though they have researched and prepared thoroughly for the interview, so impressions count.

But presentation is about more than just your appearance – anyone can make the effort to look good without buying new clothes. It's about letting the interviewer know you have tried – that you care about making a good impression, and that you take the interview seriously enough to prepare.

Is this you?

♦ People shouldn't judge by appearances. I should get the job based on what I can do, not what I look like.

♦ If I dress up for an interview, it looks too keen. I prefer to look as if I've just come from a normal day at work.

♦ Why bother? All the interviews I've had have been with people who didn't make any effort to look smart themselves!

♦ If I look too smart, everyone at work will know where I'm going – it's a bit of a give-away!

Making a good impression

Making a good impression isn't just about the clothes you wear. It's about the whole impression you give at interview. Everyone tends to focus on first impressions, and it's often said that interviewers decide within 30 seconds of meeting you whether or not they want you. Some judgements are made on a conscious level within this short timeframe, it's true, and certainly we are all subconsciously influenced by first impressions to some extent.

So what goes into this impression? It's a mixture of factors, some of which you can influence, and some you can't:

♦ physical appearance

♦ dress

♦ manner – are you friendly, relaxed and approachable?

♦ what you say

♦ how you behave

♦ neatness

♦ timekeeping

♦ attitude – enthusiastic, shy, etc

♦ personal hygiene and grooming.

Most of these factors are subjective, not objective – that is, they cannot be measured, although some of them have at least some common standard. For example, although 'smart dress' is subjective, most people have a fairly clear idea of what they would agree is smart dress. Other factors such as physical appearance are very subjective indeed.

Given that, generally speaking, presentation is based on impressions that are subjective, just how can you prepare and make sure you present yourself well in all situations? You can't – not in all situations. You might turn yourself out spotlessly for interview to find that the company has a relaxed dress policy, for example, and everyone else is in jeans and shirts. What you can do is try your best to achieve a happy medium, so that you will do well in the majority of situations.

> Presentation is based on appearance, which is often in the eye of the beholder.

What to wear

Smart dress
What is meant by 'smart dress' is subjective. Be relatively conservative, and opt for something businesslike and appropriate to the situation – obviously some jobs or fields require different styles or standards of dress.

Pay attention to detail
Details such as odd or missing buttons, socks that don't match, torn clothing, frayed edges or loose ends all detract from your image. Check your clothes carefully before you put them on.

Colour

Choose a businesslike colour. Daffodil yellow may be your favourite colour, but a more neutral shirt or blouse will probably go down better at interview. Splashes of colour, such as a colourful blouse or tie, can be stylish and they may make you more memorable and well-presented, but don't go too far. Save the more exotic components of your wardrobe for *after* you've got the job!

Shoes

Make sure that shoes are not scuffed or dirty, and that they go with the rest of your outfit. Beware of new shoes – it is easy to forget to remove those white labels from the bottom of new shoes – not a serious mistake, but someone might see them and that's not what you want to be remembered for.

Personal comfort

Never underestimate personal comfort. Looking perfect at the price of your personal comfort rarely serves any purpose. Your discomfort may show without you realising it, especially in the case of shoes that pinch or rub. Wearing something comfortable will make you more relaxed and less stressed, and will allow you to behave more naturally.

> Deciding what to wear isn't actually that difficult. But don't leave things to chance – plan in advance and check all items carefully.

Personal presentation

Hygiene

There is more to presenting a good image than what
you wear. Interviews can often be in fairly small
rooms, so things like hygiene, body odour, bad breath,
etc, *will* be noticed.

Perfume/aftershave

Beware of wearing too strong a perfume or aftershave.
It can be overpowering in a small room, or it may be
not to the interviewer's liking. At the very least, it's
unnecessary. Wear something subtle, not strong.

Grooming

Basic details like having a hair cut if necessary,
washing your hair, clean fingernails, etc, shouldn't
need mentioning, but it's surprising how many
candidates forget to check these little details and turn
up for interviews with chipped nail polish, food on
their moustache, or hair that obviously hasn't been
brushed or combed! Do make sure you build in
enough time for a quick last minute check in the
mirror before your interview begins!

Shoes and bags

Shoes and bags are easily overlooked as well. Many
candidates dressed to perfection let themselves down
with old or scuffed shoes, or simply wear shoes that
obviously have no idea what polish is! Bags can also be
old and tired – and battered briefcases don't impress

anyone by looking well used; they just look scruffy. Remember the details.

> There is more to how you look than your clothes. Your appearance can be enhanced by good dress, but no amount of smart dressing can cover up a basic hygiene or grooming problem.

Waiting

As we have said previously, plan to get there early and wait. Waiting can be more complex than you think, however.

Where to wait

Bear in mind that there may be nowhere nearby to wait. Not all businesses are conveniently situated near shops and cafés, and you may have to wait at a location ten or fifteen minutes' walk away if you want to wait in a coffee bar or café. Or you could try waiting in other places such as a local library. Ideally, you should avoid waiting at the place of the interview. Try to arrive early enough to find somewhere else to wait – somewhere you can relax and feel calm and do some last minute preparation if necessary.

Don't wait in a smoking area, or smoke immediately before your interview – some people are sensitive to cigarette smoke, and dislike it. Going into an interview smelling of cigarette smoke may be unpleasant for interviewers, particularly if the interview takes place in a small room.

If you do have to wait at the place of the interview, for example if the weather is particularly bad, or the building is in a remote location or on an industrial estate, now is the time to be nice to the receptionist! Ideally, you want to be allowed to wait, but not be announced until the correct time. Interviewers may not be impressed by interviewees who are too early – it may create the impression that you are desperate to impress.

Ask the receptionist pleasantly if there is somewhere you can wait, but say that you would prefer not to be announced until at most five minutes before your interview time. When you are ready, don't forget to remind the receptionist that you are ready – you don't want to be forgotten and make the interviewer think you're late!

Eating and drinking whilst waiting

As we said above, many interview rooms can be quite small, and not everyone likes cigarette smoke. So, if you have a quick cigarette just before the interview to calm your nerves, have it in a well ventilated place and make sure your breath is fresh afterwards!

If you are having a coffee, tea or soft drink while you wait, beware of drinking too much – an interview can often last an hour, more if there is more than one person to see. You don't want to have to visit the loo halfway through! Coffee also contains chemicals that can add to your nervousness.

Beware of alcohol. A quick drink may be ideal for relaxing you or calming your nerves, but it may lead to over-confidence, and alcohol on the breath is rarely appreciated at any interview. The smell can also linger on your clothes, as with cigarettes.

Try to avoid either eating just before an interview, or being interviewed on an empty stomach. Either may cause embarrassment, particularly if your stomach starts to make noises during the interview.

Prepare to wait

Take with you your notes, a copy of the job advert, and any other relevant literature you have and have a last-minute read through everything, so it is fresh in your mind.

Arriving early only to hang about is pointless. Plan to use waiting time to maximum effectiveness. Being busy while you wait will reduce your stress levels.

Summary points

♦ **Making a good impression is about more than the way you look.**

♦ **Choose your interview clothes and accessories carefully. It's not a fashion parade – it's about creating the right image and impression.**

♦ Don't ignore your personal presentation.

♦ Plan your journey to the interview with military precision, allowing for contingencies and waiting time.

♦ Hanging about isn't waiting. Waiting is a slot of time you can use effectively to calm and prepare yourself.

Chapter 3

Meeting and Greeting

First impressions count – there's no denying it. But they can also be changed and influenced.

In this Chapter:

♦ **arriving**
♦ **breaking the ice**
♦ **shaking hands**
♦ **accepting refreshments**
♦ **sitting down.**

There is a common saying that an interviewer decides within the first 30 seconds of meeting you whether or not he/she wants to hire you. This is unlikely to be true, especially now that managers are becoming more and more enlightened, more aware of 'human factors' such as psychology, and are better trained in interviewing techniques, etc.

However, there is no denying the fact that preconceptions and prejudices exist, as do instant reactions. People do tend to react positively or negatively to others quite quickly; to get around this at interview you have to bear in mind that you *can* influence interviewers, even to the extent of changing an initial negative reaction. Obviously, the quicker you start to influence them, the better, so the early stages of an interview are vital, when you are introducing yourself, meeting and greeting, etc.

Some people make their minds up less quickly, and are initially objective, forming their opinion of you over a longer period of time. Again, influencing them early on helps them to make the right decision about you.

Is this you?

♦ I hate it when you can see that people have prejudged you. It's not fair!

♦ This is a big deal for just getting into a room with someone – it seems over-complicated.

♦ The beginning is just when I'm *most* nervous. I don't need all these extra things to worry about.

♦ The whole meeting and greeting thing is a con trick. Let's face it, they're just trying to lull you into a false sense of security for the grilling that's to come.

Arriving

From the moment you enter . . .

You're on show right from the start:

- You may be on security camera from the moment you enter the building

- Receptionists/PAs, etc, may be asked their opinion, or what they thought of you, so be on your best behaviour with everybody from the moment you step into the building.

Remember what people look for

- People like people who are like themselves

- People like people who can initiate conversation if necessary

- People like others to respond if they initiate conversation

- People like people with confidence (but not too much!)

- People relate to people who can express themselves appropriately

Bags, coats and other baggage

- Try to avoid carrying too much baggage

- Ladies should avoid carrying both a handbag and briefcase – it's too much

- If possible, avoid carrying multiple items such as a coat and umbrella *and* briefcase into the interview

- Ask if you can leave things in reception before you are announced – it shows confidence as well as getting rid of the clutter!

♦ Discard or put away newspapers, etc before arriving

♦ If you have a file of interview information, by all means carry it so they will know you have gone to the time and trouble of preparing, but don't be too obvious about it – understated is best.

> Arriving is important – it's part of those vital first few seconds.

Breaking the ice

Start the ball rolling

Never be afraid to initiate conversation if necessary. It shows confidence without being pushy. Safe comments are things like 'It's a beautiful day, isn't it?' or 'What a lovely building; have you been here long?'

Respond appropriately

If a conversation is started, don't rush in too quickly. 'Small talk' is an appropriate phrase – most interviewers start off with a few quick and easy questions and comments to get people relaxed and comfortable. So don't give a great long explanation to a question at this stage. Keep your answers short, to the point, and positive.

Beware of negatives

Even if you have had the journey from hell to get to your interview, play things down if asked about it. Starting off on a negative footing isn't really ideal. It may not do you any harm, but it is unlikely to do you any good either. Journey and travel details are often a potential pitfall. Remember, if you get the job they will be expecting you to travel to work every day, on time. So giving the information that the journey was long or difficult isn't giving them the impression it would be easy for you to work for them! If you need to explain lateness, for example, end with a positive note, such as 'The journey coming from my current place of work was a nightmare – obviously coming here from home would be much easier.'

Body language

With body language, three things seem to make people relate to each other quickly and easily at a first meeting:

♦ Make eye contact – look them in the eye

♦ Smile – to show you are pleased to see them

♦ The 'eyebrow flash' – quickly raising your eyebrows when being introduced apparently shows interest in the other person and indicates a willingness to establish a good relationship.

The first few seconds of being introduced are actually a good opportunity to get things off on the right foot.

Shaking hands

Don't panic!

People very often dread shaking hands, and yet it's a minor thing that is usually over in a second or two. It's hard to see why people are so nervous about it. It does, however, give an important element to the impression you make in those vital first few minutes.

Sweaty palms

You may have sweaty palms. At worst, this can be obvious and unpleasant. On the other hand, it may not even be consciously noticed by the interviewer, but subconsciously you could be transmitting a signal that you are nervous. Very discreetly and without being noticed, wipe your hand before shaking your interviewer's hand. For example, you could rest your right hand on your leg when waiting, and as you stand up or step forward to shake, just run your palm over your clothes. Never be seen to wipe your hand before shaking – it shows you feel dirty and unworthy to touch them – it's very subordinate. Conversely, *never* wipe your hand after shaking someone else's – it shows you didn't like touching the other person!

The 'dead fish'

A limp handshake is sometimes known as the 'dead fish'. We've all at sometime shaken someone's hand and it's been floppy and lifeless. Feels awful, doesn't it? Don't fall into this trap yourself – hold your interviewer's hand firmly. Limp handshakes come across as unconfident. This type of handshake says:

♦ I'm not confident

♦ I don't have any character

♦ I'm not comfortable shaking hands

♦ I'm nervous.

The 'death grip'

On the other hand, don't grip someone's hand too strongly. People resent it, and it has become something of a stereotype, and may be seen as the action of an aggressive business person. It's true that some employers *want* a firm handshake, especially for sales-type roles, if they're looking for a strong character. But tread carefully – be guided by your interviewer. If your interviewer gives you a 'death grip', responding in kind will probably be the right thing to do. Too-firm handshakes, however, are definitely inappropriate for older (ie, elderly) interviewers, and some ladies – they can hurt. And if you are shaking hands with someone who's your equal, it becomes a competitive gesture. Be sensible about how strong your handshake grip is – the 'death grip' handshake says:

♦ I'm overconfident

♦ I'm competitive

♦ I'm insensitive

◆ I'm pushy

◆ I'm trying to dominate

◆ I'm trying to force my ideas

◆ I'm trying to give you a message.

The perfect handshake

◆ Engage the whole hand, palm to palm.

◆ Match the hand pressure of the other person. If they
  are a person with a firm handshake, you want to
  shake back just as firmly. For people with a weaker
  handshake you should soften your handshake grip
  in return.

◆ It shouldn't last longer than how long it takes to
  say 'One, two, three.'

◆ Accompany the handshake with a smile and eye
  contact.

Shaking hands takes no more than a second or
two, but it all adds to the interviewer's impression
of you.

Accepting refreshments

The golden rule

The golden rule is to be comfortable, so that you can
relax. So if you are desperately thirsty, of course you
should accept refreshments.

Extreme nerves

If you are so nervous you fear spilling something, politely say 'No, thank you' and decline. Better to do this than to accept in an attempt to co-operate with the interviewer and then have a catastrophe!

Check what your interviewer does

By far the safest option is to ask if the interviewer is having anything. Some people feel embarrassed if they are offered coffee and accept, and then the interviewer doesn't join them. Say something simple such as:

♦ 'I'll join you if you're having something, otherwise I'm fine, thank you.'

♦ 'Only if you're going to.'

♦ 'Are you having anything?'

Smoking and eating

Never eat in an interview, regardless of what the interviewer does. Interviews are about answering the interviewer's questions, and it's hard to talk when you are eating. You end up juggling words and mouthfuls, and it just looks clumsy.

You can see what a disaster area refreshments can be – be careful before accepting.

Sitting down

Wait your turn!

Never sit down before being invited to do so. Waiting
is not only polite, it gives a nervous interviewer
confidence, and gives them the lead.

Be alert and interested

The aim in an interview is to appear alert and
interested. You can't do this if you are slumped. Lean
slightly forward – not too much or you will look odd!
Sit up straight.

Stay relaxed

Stay relaxed but not slumped. Sitting uncomfortably
and bolt upright may look great at first, but after 30
minutes it may be so uncomfortable that your whole
body language changes – the interviewer isn't a
mindreader and he/she may decide you aren't happy
with the job or the company if you *look* unhappy.

Do something with your hands

Oddly enough, when sitting down, one of the hardest
things to do is to decide what to do with your hands!
Don't dangle them off the arms of the chair – it's odd.
And don't clutch them together, which looks nervous.
Find a relaxed way of holding them or laying them on
your legs.

Territory and positioning

You may get to choose where to sit, or the interviewer
may direct you to a seat. This positioning is rarely

random – so choose your territory carefully. Don't sit facing a bright light, or with the sun in your eyes. If possible don't sit directly opposite the interviewer face-to-face, looking directly at each other – it's confrontational and may make some interviewers feel uncomfortable. Try to sit at an angle to them if at all possible. You can easily do this by moving your chair very slightly as you sit down, so you are positioned at a slight angle to them.

Avoid closed body language

Avoid folding your arms and crossing your legs – closing your body language. It says you are unreceptive and not willing to listen.

> How you sit says a lot to the interviewer, and subconsciously it will be adding to their opinion of you.

Summary points

♦ **Remember you may be noticed from the second you enter the building.**

♦ **Breaking the ice may be something you have to initiate.**

♦ **Shaking hands appropriately takes only a few seconds but adds to the image you are presenting.**

♦ Accept refreshments where necessary and/or appropriate.

♦ Even something as simple as the way in which you sit down can convey a message to the interviewer.

Chapter 4

Handling Nerves

Being nervous isn't just a rotten feeling to have to experience – it can ruin your chances of giving your best performance as well!

In this Chapter:

- **handling emotions**
- **transforming thought processes**
- **relaxing and calming yourself**
- **emergency measures.**

Being nervous can be a pretty unpleasant feeling. Nobody likes to feel anxious, under-confident, fearful of the situation, unsure of themselves – but most people have experienced one or more of these feelings at some time or other.

But the risk of feeling bad isn't the only problem. Uncontrolled nervousness can alter your behaviour, your body language and what you say – when you feel nervous you can behave differently to how you usually behave. And interviews are doubly difficult because both you and the interviewer may be nervous.

Controlling your nerves isn't easy, and even if it were, it's one more thing to have to think about in what is an inherently stressful situation. But keeping your anxiety under control can reap huge benefits and nerves *can* be controlled, so it is worth trying. Learning simple techniques will at first help, and eventually may even become an unconscious habit, so you automatically control your nerves better with practice.

Is this you?

♦ I hate interviews. I never do well, and I never will. What's the point?

♦ I don't believe you can ever really control nerves – some people are just more nervous than others and that's that.

♦ It's all right for interviewers – they don't get nervous.

♦ If I spend all my time controlling my nerves, how will I be able to concentrate on the interview itself and on doing myself justice?

Handling emotions

Thoughts versus emotions

With nerves, is it really your emotions that are a problem? In many ways, the problem is more often a thought process than an actual emotion. Let me explain: thoughts and emotions are not the same. For example:

THOUGHT	EMOTION GENERATED
'This is a scary situation'	Fear
'I might not get the job'	Nervousness or anxiety
'Damn, I messed that up!'	Hopelessness
'I should have said X instead . . .'	Frustration

Controlling emotions

As you can see, it is actually thoughts that generate emotions. Someone who feels fear, anxiety, nervousness, hopelessness, frustration, etc, would find it very difficult to do anything about it – and that's perfectly natural. But just how do you *stop* being afraid?

The problem is that once the emotion is there, it's happening, and very hard to stop. Often these emotions produce complex hormonal or chemical reactions in the body, and controlling reactions is next to impossible. The key to controlling any emotion – such as nervousness, for example – is to remember that it is caused by a thought process. Disrupt the thought process and you cut off the stimulus that causes the emotion.

Thoughts and emotions are not the same at all. You can influence your thoughts, but your emotions are a reaction to them.

Transforming thought processes

Internal dialogue

For nervousness, you need to identify the thought process behind your nervousness and so deal with it more positively. You do this by internal dialogue. Discuss the thought process with yourself, and try just focusing on the thoughts – that will take your attention away from the emotion and its biological effects on your system. Don't worry that you won't have time for this – conducting internal dialogue is pretty quick for most people; these split-second 'conversations' usually go on in our heads all the time.

Identify thought processes

♦ Identify the thought process, eg, 'I might not get the job.'

♦ Doing this takes your mind off the emotion you are feeling.

♦ It also refocuses your attention.

Evaluate rationally

♦ Evaluate the thought *rationally* – this means examining it unemotionally.

- Is it justified to that extent?

- Is it even true?

- Would the consequences that you fear really be all that bad?

- Talk it over with yourself – *rationally*, eg, 'They wouldn't have interviewed me if they didn't think I was a possibility. If I don't get it, there are other jobs out there. But I might get it – who knows?'

Replace the negative thought with something more helpful

- amend it

- replace with a more sensible, appropriate and/or positive thought, eg, 'I might get the job or I might not. Either way this is valuable experience I can learn from.'

Re-examine how you feel

- Re-examine the emotion you feel

- It should either be reducing or gone, eg, 'Hey! If I see it as a learning experience, this interview doesn't make me feel quite so nervous!'

Amending the thought processes behind emotions helps us to control unwanted emotions such as nervousness.

Relaxing and calming yourself

Breathe

♦ Getting oxygen to your brain will make you able to think more clearly.

♦ Breathe deeply and slowly.

♦ Try breathing in for a count of five, then out for a count of five.

♦ Get some fresh air. Like breathing, this will increase the supply of oxygen to your brain and make you able to think better.

♦ Take a short walk – for the same reason.

Calming rituals

♦ People often have calming rituals, such as having a cup of tea. If you don't have one, establish one!

♦ Have a drink – preferably a soft drink, juice or water.

♦ Remember that tea and coffee are stimulants, so if you are very nervous, they won't help and could even make things worse – caffeine can make you feel even more anxious!

Relaxing yourself

♦ Find somewhere to sit down.

♦ Concentrate on relaxing.

♦ Starting with your feet and moving up, tighten each part of your body in turn and then relax it. This will remove any muscle tension.

♦ Concentrate on relaxing your body – stop nervous, edgy movements and actions such as fiddling, licking your lips, biting lips, tapping feet, etc.

Relaxing and calming yourself is something you need to do physically. Just the act of physically concentrating on changing things helps your mind focus on something constructive and positive, and will reduce nervousness.

Emergency measures

Keep things in proportion

♦ You are not alone. Everyone dries up at some stage.

♦ Sometimes the physical effects of anxiety can affect the vocal chords and make it hard to speak. Or you get so nervous you don't know *what* to say.

♦ Panicking will only make things worse.

Buy yourself some time

♦ Ask for a glass of water.

♦ Not only will the water help, but the time it takes to get it for you will buy you some breathing space so you can collect your thoughts.

♦ Use this to try to relax.

♦ Pause in your conversation, or when asked a question. Count to five then continue. This doesn't sound as odd as you might think – pausing to gather your thoughts is a natural thing, and people often do it.

♦ Ask for thinking time. You can always say 'Can I have a minute to think this one through?'

♦ If you're asked a difficult question, ask if you can come back to it. It's not ideal, but can be acceptable. For example, you might say, 'Sorry, can we come back to that question in a few minutes?'

Refocus on something else

♦ Stop thinking about being nervous, and start thinking about relaxing.

♦ Refocus your attention – use some of the internal dialogue technique we have previously discussed.

Come clean and ask for help

♦ Admit it! Admitting honestly to being nervous can help the interviewer carry out the interview. There is nothing wrong with saying honestly (but not in a grovelling way) something such as 'I'm sorry – I'm actually quite nervous about this interview, as I really like the look of this job.' Giving a positive reason for your nervousness will make you seem less like a shrinking violet.

Everyone gets nervous at times. Being able to control this and turn it to your advantage can help your performance greatly, as well as making you feel a whole lot better!

Summary points

♦ Learn that emotions can be handled – they aren't something that you are totally at the mercy of, something you can only suffer until they go away.

♦ The key to handling emotions is to identify and amend the thought processes that underlie them. This is done by internal dialogue.

♦ Learn physical mechanisms that help to relax and calm you – and use them.

♦ Remember that you can cope with an emergency, by resorting to emergency measures.

Chapter 5

Body Language

Body language is a huge subject. Understanding it can make life a lot easier, as it can add greatly to the image you present to an interviewer.

In this Chapter:

♦ **the golden rule**
♦ **gestures and meanings**
♦ **eye contact**
♦ **listening skills**
♦ **mirroring**
♦ **disagreeing.**

Body language is a huge subject upon which many books have been written. Unfortunately, they can sometimes give you conflicting advice, and studying body language in depth can mean you spend all your time studying other people's mannerisms instead of concentrating on your own! You need to have enough information to allow you to focus on performing at your best at interview. Knowing the basics of body language can increase your performance at interview greatly. Being able to control your own body language makes it easier for you to relate to interviewers, and to make a good impression. It can also make you appear more confident, more honest, and more in tune with the interviewer.

But there is one other advantage of knowing about body language – it helps you control your nerves, if you suffer from nervousness. Concentrating on your physical actions will take your attention away from negative thought processes and feeling nervous, and make you focus instead on what you are actually doing. This can reduce your nervousness significantly.

Is this you?

♦ I can't be bothered with body language – I already have a million things to think about in an interview!

♦ Everyone knows about body language now so it's irrelevant. We all know what things mean, so there's no big secret advantage to knowing it any more.

♦ I think all the advice I've ever seen on body language is just false – it just makes people look silly, as if they're acting.

♦ I know the basics and what not to do – but can you really use body language to make an interviewer like you more?

The golden rule

The golden rule with body language is to match your interviewer's body language. Like attracts like.

Match verbal with non-verbal behaviours

♦ Use non-verbal behaviour – ie, body language, to reinforce and back up what you are saying verbally.

♦ Try never to use body language that gives a different message from your verbal message, such as saying 'Yes' and shaking your head at the same time, or a more common example, saying 'No' and nodding.

♦ The trick is to always match non-verbal messages with verbal messages – so you should always nod when you agree, shake your head when you are disagreeing, etc.

Mismatching

So what happens if you mismatch – if you literally do say 'yes' and at the same time shake your head? (Try it – it's actually quite hard to do!) Research varies, but almost every piece of research that has been carried out on the subject shows that the *non-verbal* signal will come through strongest. So the non-verbal signal will be the one believed, and the other person may reject the content of your words, or they will not even notice the words at all, but will end up feeling you've said what your non-verbal signal said!

Other types of matching

There are other ways in which you can use the principle of matching, that like attracts like. These will be explained later, but in particular, a technique called 'mirroring' is useful. This is where you match, or mirror, the other person's body language, which almost always has the effect of making the person you're talking to feel more in rapport with you – they relate to you better.

Like attracts like. People like people like them. People relate better to people they feel 'in synch' with. This is one of the fundamental aspects of body language.

Gestures and meanings

As we have said, an amazing number of books on body language have been published. Listing the things you can do to convey certain meanings isn't always helpful, as it will give you too much to think about in a situation which we know is inherently stressful.

Instead, here are some of the main impressions you may give to an interviewer, and some of the main signals by which your body language conveys these impressions. Choose which ones to practise and which ones to avoid – that way, you can focus on improving just one area at a time, which won't overload you!

Defensiveness

These actions convey the impression that you have something to hide:

♦ crossing or folding your arms

♦ sitting at too much of an angle to the interviewer, so you have to turn your head to look at him/her

♦ pointing your finger when making a point

♦ using your hand in a 'karate chop' gesture when making a point

♦ looking down when speaking

♦ not making eye contact.

Suspicious and distrusting

These actions suggest you are distrusting:

♦ crossing or folding your arms

♦ looking at your interviewer from underneath your eyebrows

♦ looking at your interviewer sideways – out of the corner of your eye (usually caused by sitting too much at an angle to him/her)

♦ rubbing your eyes

♦ frowning

♦ touching nose or face

♦ rubbing the back of the neck.

Nervousness

All these convey nervousness:

♦ pinching your skin

♦ fidgeting

♦ jiggling the contents of your pockets

♦ running your tongue along the front of your teeth

♦ clearing your throat

♦ running your fingers through your hair

♦ wringing your hands

♦ biting on pens or other objects

♦ twiddling your thumbs

♦ biting your fingernails (both the action itself and evidence of it)

♦ tongue-clicking

♦ gritting your teeth

♦ biting your lips.

Positive body language

All these actions, on the other hand, will enable you to establish a good rapport with interviewer:

♦ good eye contact

♦ leaning forward slightly in your chair

- tilting your head whilst maintaining eye contact with your interviewer

- open-lipped smiling

- open hands with palms visible

- unbuttoning your coat or jacket upon being seated

- keeping your chin up

- putting tips of fingers of one hand against the tips of fingers of other hand in the 'praying' or 'steepling' position

- having your hands joined behind back your when standing.

Body language can be a lot to take in and master. Concentrate on identifying the bad habits and eliminating them, and add a few good ones.

Eye contact

The importance of eye contact

- Eye contact is important as it conveys confidence and trust.

- It establishes a rapport with the other person – ie, a link, a connection or relationship between you.

♦ When speaking to someone, establishing eye contact allows you to check that they understand and are still interested in what you are saying.

♦ When listening, establishing eye contact conveys your attention and is a gesture of politeness.

♦ Lack of eye contact shows evasiveness, and makes it almost impossible to establish rapport with someone.

Eye contact when listening

There are two ways of looking at eye contact – either as a listener or as a speaker. As a listener, you need to make a great deal more eye contact – it's simply more appropriate for a listener to do so, and to extend your eye contact for longer periods of time than if you are speaking.

Eye contact when speaking

On the other hand, if you are a speaker, your listener will end up feeling uncomfortable if you maintain complete eye contact with them for too long. About five to ten seconds of eye contact is about right for making a connection with your listener. After that you should make your eye contact less complete and look away. Otherwise, the connection with your listener becomes too intense, and can start to feel like a staring match. Speakers tend therefore to make and break eye contact regularly, whereas listeners tend to keep eye contact for extended periods of time.

Excessive eye contact

Excessive or inappropriate eye contact will prevent you from establishing a good rapport with your interviewer:

♦ eye contact that is too strong can be too intense

♦ it can become a battle of wills

♦ it can be intimidating

♦ it can be over-familiar

♦ holding eye contact for too long can make the person speaking uncomfortable

♦ it can make you look stupid as a listener (as if you are a zombie drinking in every word!)

♦ glancing away occasionally is perfectly acceptable, so long as you restore contact quickly.

Eye contact is probably the most important element of body language. It can make or break the rapport between people in a very short time.

Listening skills

Active listening

Listening isn't just something you do with your ears! It is something you have to do actively in an interview – you don't just have to listen, you have to be *seen* to be listening. This is active listening. Listening signals or behaviours include:

- making eye contact

- nodding

- making 'listening noises' ('Mmm', 'Uh-huh', etc)

- smiling

- leaning forward

- open body language

- tilting the head to one side

- reacting to what your interviewer is saying.

Concentration

The easiest way to listen properly is purely and simply to concentrate on what the person is saying! This tends to make most people exhibit at least some of the signs of active listening listed above.

Questioning

There are other, non-body language ways you can enhance your listening skills. A good way of either showing you have been listening or checking your understanding is to ask questions. You don't necessarily need to interrupt – wait until they pause or stop, and then off you go; it's your turn. Try 'Can I just check I got that correctly . . . ?'

Reflecting

Reflecting is repeating back what you just heard, in a way that isn't obvious. It checks your understanding is correct, and also shows them you understood. It also means that you are telling them what they just told you – and remember that people like people who are like them – it will add to the matching effect you are trying to create. Here are some reflecting phrases:

♦ 'So what you're saying is . . . ?'

♦ 'So you think . . . ?'

♦ 'Then would you agree that . . . ?'

♦ I agree. It *is* important that . . .'.

Listening is an active, not passive process. It is a good opportunity to relax and make a good impression at the same time.

Mirroring

What is mirroring?
Mirroring is when you imitate someone else's body language. It is like reflecting, except that reflecting is a means of establishing a rapport with someone verbally, whereas mirroring is its non-verbal equivalent. It is basically copying someone else's body language.

Why mirror?

♦ people like people like themselves

♦ it helps you establish a rapport with your interviewer

♦ it establishes a connection between you and your interviewer

♦ it strengthens any connection or rapport between you that may already exist.

A word of caution

Mirroring is something that many books on body language refer to. But many attempts at mirroring go badly wrong, as this is a very subtle technique. You need to mirror very carefully and gently, so it isn't at all obvious, otherwise you will look very strange indeed! Remember:

♦ never mirror aggressive interviewers

♦ don't mirror nervous people

♦ don't mirror bad habits like scratching

♦ only mirror people who themselves have good body language

♦ don't overdo it! – be very, very, subtle

♦ if you make it obvious that you are mirroring, you have failed.

Mirroring gestures

Mirroring *gestures* is where many people go wrong – it's simply too obvious. If someone smiles, smiling back is mirroring, but it also looks perfectly natural. But crossing your legs as soon as the other person does can look ludicrous.

♦ Don't mirror immediately – leave a gap of a few seconds.

♦ Don't mirror exactly – you could mirror crossed legs by crossing your ankles, for example.

♦ Be subtle – mirror reduced versions of what your interviewer is doing; For example, you could mirror their running a hand through their hair by just brushing back your fringe or tucking your hair behind one ear.

♦ Remember you don't have to produce an exact mirror image – if your interviewer leans to the left, wait a short while then lean either to the left or right yourself – it is the leaning you are mirroring, not its precise direction.

Mirroring is very effective for establishing rapport and contact with the interviewer. Unfortunately, it is very hard to do subtly, and many people end up looking foolish.

Disagreeing

Your right to an opinion

Interviewers are in charge during an interview situation, and it's true that they do control whether or not you get the job. But that doesn't mean you have to agree with everything they say – it might curry favour, but it may be against what you really believe, and may even make you look weak.

Tell the truth, and if you disagree with something the interviewer says, don't be afraid to say so – nicely! Most people would rather someone stood up for themselves than agreed with everything. Plus, there is always the chance that the interviewer is merely testing you – saying something they *expect* you to disagree with, to see whether or not you have the strength of character to do so.

You may also find that if you agree with them because you think it will look better, later on – in the interview or afterwards – it becomes apparent that you have been 'found out'. It's far better never to be dishonest, and so there *will* be occasions when you need to be true to yourself and disagree with an interviewer.

Question before disagreeing

If you disagree with something your interviewer says, check your understanding first. Ask a question or questions to clarify his/her meaning, before saying you disagree. It is far better to make sure you didn't misunderstand before you put your cards on the table.

Be surprised to disagree

Obviously, some people are concerned about disagreeing with an interviewer, as they don't want to give a bad impression. A good way to counteract this is to show surprise when you disagree – as if you expected to agree with the other person, thus creating an impression of how similar you are – good old matching again! Say you're surprised, and use body language to reinforce what you are saying, by raising your eyebrows and saying, for example:

♦ 'Well, I've always been in favour of . . . myself.'

♦ 'I'm surprised – I actually don't find that myself.'

♦ 'How strange – I found them/it very helpful.'

♦ 'That's interesting, because I haven't found that to be the case.'

Don't lie

Don't fall into the trap of lying and agreeing for the sake of it. If you get found out, you will have shown yourself to be dishonest, and that is one thing interviewers hate!

Disagree graciously

One reason why people don't want to disagree with things that are said to them in interviews is because they don't want to be confrontational. Disagree politely and graciously, and there should be no problem. Apologising for disagreeing (without grovelling!) is easy and doesn't seem too submissive:

'I'm sorry, I don't agree. I've always thought that . . .'

Disagreeing isn't always a complete 'no-no' with interviewers. Better to stand up for yourself and disagree without confrontation than to be caught out in a lie later.

Summary points

♦ Remember the golden rule – people like people like themselves. Matching where possible to establish common ground and rapport is your aim.

♦ Beware of using negative body language and try to make a positive impression on your interviewer by using positive body language.

♦ Eye contact is absolutely critical. But don't overdo it, and make sure you use listening or speaking eye contact as appropriate.

♦ Listening needs to be an active process, so don't just sit there – You need to be seen to be listening!

♦ Mirroring is something that is hard to do properly. Leave well alone unless you are confident in your ability to do it well.

♦ Disagreeing with your interviewer is fine so long as you do it appropriately, and aren't in any way confrontational or aggresive.

Chapter 6

Answering Questions

People get very hung up about being questioned at interview. It's not actually the biggest problem you'll have to tackle in your interview, and let's face it, you should know the answers if you are being asked about yourself!

In this Chapter:

◆ **understanding good questions**
◆ **dealing with bad questions**
◆ **correcting mistakes**
◆ **reinforcing your message.**

Being questioned about your CV, your skills and experience is the real core of an interview. Only by doing this can the interviewer establish whether or not you are a good fit with the requirements of the position for which you are being interviewed.

Everyone attending an interview expects to be questioned. Perhaps that is why answering questions gets blown up out of all proportion in many people's minds, and why they get so worked up about finding good answers to them.

The bulk of questions in any interview will be about you – what you've done, how you think and behave, what you think and feel. There is no reason why anyone should worry about answering this sort of question, as you know yourself (and therefore the answers) better than anybody! But what concerns everyone is how to present those answers in the best possible light – how to make yourself look really good at interview. Understanding questions and answers can help here.

Is this you?

◆ I hate interviews. I just feel like I'm being interrogated, no matter how nice they are.

◆ I know my own life, but I just panic when the questions start – some people word them so awkwardly I can't tell what they really want me to say!

◆ Anyone can answer a simple question – it's getting it just right so I look better than the others that counts.

◆ If the interviewers knew how to ask questions better it would be easier! Half the time I can't answer the question, because it isn't what they actually want to know . . . .

Understanding good questions

The aim of an interviewer is to get you to tell them

what they need to know, in order to make their decision. They need to get you to talk, so they can listen and pick out the information they need. So the aim of any question isn't necessarily to 'catch you out', it's simply to get you to talk to them!

Good questions

There are three main types of 'good questions':

♦ open questions

♦ probing questions

♦ forced choice questions.

Open questions

These are questions with no set answer, which force you to talk freely. For example:

♦ 'Tell me about your time at . . .'

♦ 'Talk me through your last three jobs.'

♦ 'Tell me a little bit more about . . .'

♦ 'What do you think you gained from that?'

Probing questions

These are questions which force you to go into a little more detail. They require less of an answer, but a more specific answer. Probing questions tend to use the words:

♦ 'Who . . . ?'

- 'What . . . ?'

- 'Where . . . ?'

- 'When . . . ?'

- 'How . . . ?'

- 'Why . . . ?'

Forced choice questions

Forced choice questions are designed to put you on the spot. They force you to make a choice of answer. As questions they are actually not as good as the other two types, as they can often be answered with one or two words, or even a 'Yes' or 'No', which doesn't really encourage you to talk. For this reason they are usually followed up with a probing question, such as 'Why?' or 'Could you explain that?' Here are some examples of forced choice questions:

- 'Did you enjoy that type of work or not?'

- 'Do you prefer tasks in stages or whole projects to get on with?'

- 'Are you very organised or more spontaneous?'

- 'Do you get more satisfaction from team work or achieving something alone?'

Good questions are designed to make you talk, so try to give full answers, not just a couple of words. Explain without being asked to – it helps the interviewer.

Dealing with bad questions

Bad questions are questions that close you down, and make it easy for you to say very little. They are also questions that don't actually give the interviewer any useful information about you or your suitability for the job. Good interviewers don't ask bad questions, but here are some of the types of bad questions you may be asked at interview.

Closed questions

Closed questions are poor interview technique because they only require a very short or simple 'Yes' or 'No' answer. They 'close you down' and either prevent you from saying very much, or let weak candidates get away without elaborating their answers. But occasionally an interviewer may use them deliberately, for example when short of time or if you have been giving long answers.Here are some examples:

♦ 'Did you like working there?'

♦ 'How many staff did you have?'

♦ 'Were you there long?'

If you are asked a closed question, deal with it by answering in a reasonable amount of depth anyway – as if the interviewer had asked you to expand your answers.

Leading questions

Leading questions are questions that tell you exactly what answer the interviewer wants you to give. Asking leading questions is bad because it enables weak candidates to get away with doing fairly well at interview – as they can guess what the interviewer wants them to say! It's also bad for strong candidates, as it makes it hard for them to disagree with the interviewer without knowing that this will be unexpected and unwelcome. Here are some examples of leading questions:

♦ 'So you liked it there?'

♦ 'I've always thought X, don't you agree?'

♦ 'I assume you left because . . .'

♦ 'That was a pretty senior role, wasn't it?'

Deal with leading questions by standing up for yourself. Try the 'Yes, but . . .' approach – it could work well for you.

Multiple questions

Multiple questions are where the interviewer asks several questions at once. They are bad questions because they confuse candidates, and make it hard for them to create a good impression by giving the interviewer the information he/she wants. Here are some examples of multiple questions:

♦ 'Did you like working there? They're fairly laid back, aren't they?'

♦ 'What would you choose, why would that particularly be your first choice, and do you foresee any particular problems?'

♦ 'Why did you leave there – I imagine it must have been a wrench – didn't you work there for quite some time?'

Deal with multiple questions by answering all parts of the question if possible. Organise your thoughts by numbering the questions, for example: 'Firstly, I didn't, and secondly, that was because . . .'. It will help you remember to answer all the questions within the question. If you lose track, just ask politely for them to repeat the question: often they will make it easier to understand the second time around.

Hypothetical questions

Hypothetical questions make you use your imagination. That may not sound terribly bad, but it means you aren't being allowed to give the interviewer facts, only conjecture. It can often indicate a weak interviewer, and yet these questions are all too common. Here are some examples:

♦ 'What do you think you would do if . . . ?'

♦ 'How would you handle a customer who . . . ?'

♦ 'If you had been in charge, how would you have handled it?'

♦ 'Why do you think we put that in the advert?'

To stand out from other candidates, deal with hypothetical questions by treating them as if they were asking for facts anyway. 'Well, when I worked at X I had to do that, and I handled it like this . . .'. This will make you stand out from weak candidates who are speaking from guesswork and imagination, not demonstrating experience and skill.

> Interviewers aren't all fantastic and experienced at asking questions – you may need to help them out, by dealing well with bad questions.

Correcting mistakes

It's not strictly speaking answering questions, but at some stage in an interview, you may well find yourself having to correct a mistake. For example, you may be asked a question which isn't accurate: 'Presumably you've worked with . . . before?' Or, you may be in the interview and suddenly it becomes apparent that the interviewer has got something wrong.

Deal with mistakes immediately

When there is an obvious mistake, deal with it immediately. Letting it go out of politeness may seem the safest option – in the short term, it is. After all, it might be just a slip of the tongue, such as referring to the wrong company or something minor like calling you Mark instead of Mike.

On the other hand, it could be a much more significant mistake – the interviewer may have totally got the wrong idea about something. Letting it go can be dangerous because it may come up again. And the longer you let the interviewer go on believing something and saying it without being corrected, the more confusing it is for the interviewer when you eventually correct him/her.

How to interrupt

If an interviewer makes a mistake, the best way to deal with it is to interrupt him/her. Interrupting is usually a negative behaviour, and something that you should avoid, but in this instance, you need to nip things gently in the bud, and correct any apparent mistake immediately. Here are some tips on how to do it:

♦ Interrupt gently. Interrupting is normally regarded as negative behaviour, so make sure you do it politely.

♦ Apologise for interrupting: 'Sorry, but . . .' People often say that apologising makes you look weak and submissive, but it is perfectly all right to apologise (without making a huge issue of it) if you are interrupting someone – in fact under these circumstances, it's appropriate.

♦ Make eye contact. Look at the interviewer when interrupting him/her – it grabs his/her attention.

♦ Raise your hand slightly, palm towards them. This is a 'stopping signal' in body language, and makes it easier for them to stop and listen to you. It shouldn't be a dramatic gesture like a policeman directing traffic, or like a schoolboy asking teacher a question – just a slight movement is all that is necessary.

♦ Point out the interviewer's error politely: 'Sorry, but it was actually XYZ Ltd, not ABC Limited where I did . . .'.

♦ Smile – it never does any harm!

> Nip misconceptions in the bud before they continue. You are building up a picture with the interviewer, and you need to make sure it is a correct one.

Reinforcing your message

Sometimes you may feel you have not said, or been given the chance to say, exactly what you wanted to say. You may want to reinforce your message.

Convincing people by body language

There are certain ways you can convince an interviewer you are telling the truth:

♦ eye contact – meet their gaze steadily and don't look away

♦ hand on heart – touch your heart or chest when making an important point

♦ nod whilst you speak.

Strengthening and emphasising your message

◆ Reinforce your message by repeating it – not too
emphatically, just say it then repeat it once.

◆ Reflect back what they say then lead on from there
to make your own point. For example: 'I know
you've said the job is mainly working on X, so I'd
like to make sure you realise just how experienced
at this I am.'

> Convincing people of the major points you are
> trying to make can make the difference between
> an average interview and a performance that will
> be remembered.

Summary points

◆ **Good questions are easy to answer, so use the
time to relax and enjoy yourself! Listen carefully
and answer the question.**

◆ **Help the interviewer. Poor questioning
technique makes it easy for candidates
to give poor answers. Read between the
lines and give them the information you think
they seek, however badly they phrase the
question.**

◆ **Ask for clarification if you need to.**

♦ When you need to correct an interviewer's mistakes, be polite but factual. Don't just let it go – it may cause problems later.

♦ Be honest and truthful, and use body language to impress on the interviewer that you are doing so where necessary.

Chapter 7

Leave on a Good Note

You'll never make a good first impression on your way out of an interview! But what you can do is blow a good performance by leaving on a low note, or worse, creating a last-minute negative impression.

In this Chapter:

♦ **saying goodbye**
♦ **being remembered**
♦ **final points.**

We have said that the impression people get of you when you first meet can be lasting and very important. Similarly, when you part, you can either reinforce a good impression or ruin all your good work – people do tend to remember the last thing you said or did.

You know the issues about standing up, shaking hands, what to say etc, that we looked at in earlier chapters. Oddly, the relief that you can feel when a stressful interview is over can also affect your behaviour and co-ordination, as your body releases a flood of new hormones and chemicals into your body's bloodstream.

Stay cool and polished until out of sight and earshot of your interviewer – manage your exit in the same way you managed your entrance, and everything will be fine. But you can also use the last few minutes or seconds of your interview to enhance your chances with a good positive sales pitch.

Is this you?

♦ When it's over, I can't wait to get out of there! I can't be bothered with anything but getting away as quickly as possible so I can relax.

♦ I hate that awkward couple of minutes at the end when you're both 'wrapping things up'. I never know what to do.

♦ You can't prepare for the end of an interview – it all depends how well it's gone.

♦ If the first impression counts for so much, why worry about what happens on the way out?

Saying goodbye

The interviewer will usually signal that the interview is at an end.

What to do

♦ Stay seated until the interviewer gets up.

♦ But gather your things together, so there aren't any awkward pauses when you're ready to leave.

♦ Try to avoid grabbing a hasty last mouthful of water or coffee – it looks rushed and rather odd.

What to say

♦ Let the interviewer say 'Goodbye' then respond appropriately.

♦ If he/she doesn't, take the initiative and just say 'Goodbye' politely.

♦ Compliment them (but not excessively!) by saying, for example: 'It was nice to meet you', or 'It's been a pleasure.'

♦ Shake hands. If they don't offer their hand, offer yours first.

♦ Remember what we have said about handshakes. Even if you feel you've done badly, offer a handshake that is confident.

Leaving the room and building

♦ Keep up your best behaviour until you are out of the interviewer's sight and hearing.

♦ Remember: you never know who may be around, so be careful to stay professional until you leave the building – you may be on a security camera!

♦ Don't forget to say 'Goodbye . . . and thank you!' to receptionists.

Interviewers may need help closing the interview – many of them find this the most difficult part, so you may have to take the initiative!

Being remembered

Prepare good questions

At the end of an interview, you will usually be asked whether you have any questions. Prepare some in advance to make sure you always have one or two, as this helps to make interviewers think you are seriously interested in the job.

On the other hand, don't go in with a long list – it's daunting for interviewers and puts them on the spot. Just think of a maximum of, say, three questions. It's fine to write them down, but don't make a shopping list!

Smile and be charming

If you have made any mistakes, or if you have been very serious and professional during the rest of the interview, this is the time when you can now smile and appear a little more relaxed. Often, interviewers who have been nervous will relax at this point too, so this may be a good chance to find out more about the company as the atmosphere starts to relax at last.

You want to leave the impression that you would be a good part of the organisation's team, so you want to appear likeable. If you are now asking questions, be especially friendly. The interviewer has been in charge up to this point, asking all the questions. Suddenly, this can be where you get to put him/her on the spot, so be nice about it as he/she can feel under pressure. You want him/her to feel comfortable with you after you have left.

Questions *not* to ask

♦ 'How did I do?' (or any words to that effect). This shows lack of confidence and you may not have done that badly.

♦ 'Is X a problem?' Don't ever highlight problems on the way out. Better by far to hope they have forgotten X (a bad point) and instead highlight Y (your good point) in some way.

♦ 'If I don't get this job can you keep me in mind for anything else?' (or words to that effect!). This just makes you look desperate for work, and it won't do you any favours.

Raise concerns and deal with them

If you think the interviewer has any unstated concerns, or if he/she has expressed any, try to deal with them. For example, an interviewer might say to you that he/she is not sure whether or not your skillset would fit within the team, but that he/she wants to interview several people to see who would be the best fit with their requirements. At the end of the interview, you could address this issue if you felt it would help create or reinforce a positive impression: 'I remember you mentioned the team fit. Can I just say that the team you described is very similar to the one I'm in at present, and I'm sure I could adapt to any differences quickly.'

Obviously, this is a matter for your personal judgement – the golden rule is to finish on a positive note, and to raise nothing negative at the end of your interview.

When it is your turn to ask questions, don't try to interview the interviewer – he/she won't like it!

Final points

Putting right things that have gone wrong

If anything went badly, such as you being late, or misunderstanding a question completely, bring it up again and put it right if you can. Obviously, if you can't put it right, don't raise it, or you will end on a negative, but where you can, do so: 'I'm so sorry I misinterpreted what you were saying. I hope you'll be able to see now that actually I've got quite a lot of experience at X.'

Having the last word

If you can prepare a few 'parting shots' that are really positive, commit them to memory so you can use whichever seems most appropriate on the day. For example: 'It's been a pleasure to meet you – I've really enjoyed learning more about what you do.'

What *not* to say

- 'I really hope to hear from you.'

- 'Please don't forget to let me know about the outcome.'

- 'Sorry for being late!' (Don't remind them about bad points at this stage)

- 'Good luck with the other interviews!'

- 'I hope you find the right person.' (Remember, you should assume *you* are the right person – that's the image you want to cultivate.)

- 'Thank you for seeing me.'

> This is your very, very last chance to make a good impression. Never jeopardise it by saying anything negative.

Summary points

- **Saying a good goodbye is almost as important as making a good greeting. Plan it carefully in advance.**

♦ Make sure you are remembered by preparing a couple of short 'closers', using the ones that are most appropriate at the time.

♦ Always leave on a positive note; never ever leave on a negative note.

HOW TO WRITE AN IMPRESSIVE CV & COVER LETTER

A comprehensive guide for the UK job seeker

TRACEY WHITMORE

Includes a free CD with templates and real-life examples

Your CV and cover letter are your first communication with a prospective employer. As the job market has become increasingly competitive, making the right first impression has never been more important. If you compromise on the quality of your CV and cover letter, you greatly reduce your chances of winning an interview.

This book, which will appeal to anyone from entry level to board level, encompasses a step-by-step guide on how to achieve killer competitive advantage by producing a thoroughly impressive CV and cover letter. The job acquisition process, which has changed significantly in recent years, is discussed fully, and really effective job-hunting tactics are provided.

- Interviews undertaken with top HR professionals, who are often the first point of entry, outline what you need to do to impress them. Their views and opinions are provided throughout the book.

- The book and CD are packed with practical examples of CVs and cover letters that have actually worked in real-life. These individuals were struggling to win interviews prior to their CV revamp. Their new CVs secured several interviews, many of which resulted in job offers.

- The CD contains CV and cover letter templates, and full transcripts of interviews held with twelve industry experts from blue chip employers such as Vodafone, Tesco, KPMG, Korn Ferry and Jonathan Wren.

ISBN 978-1-84528-365-0

WHY SHOULD I WORK FOR YOU?

How to find the job that`s right for you – and get the offer

KEITH POTTS AND JASON DEIGN

This book starts from the premise that in today's uncertain job market you, not your employer, call the shots in your career. Packed with tips, exercises and case studies, it will give you all you need to create a 'you-shaped job' and set the course for a better life. Discover: the four things you need to get any job; a unique way of working out which job you should be doing; six ways to get more money out of your current employer even if they won't give you a pay rise; how to avoid pitfalls in job hunting and interviews; how to create a life-long plan that will help you enjoy a happy and fulfilling career for the rest of your working days. Author, Keith Potts is an acknowledged expert on employment practices and trends as a result of his role as founder and managing director of Jobsite UK, one of the UK's leading commercial Internet recruitment services.

ISBN 978-1-84528-347-6

HOW TO ANSWER HARD INTERVIEW QUESTIONS

CHARLIE GIBBS

'Allows us to actually get inside the head of an interviewer and explore in detail the hundreds of questions he or she may pose to us on the day. Written in a no-nonsense conversational style this book covers everything you need to know about an interview - before, during and after the interview.' *www.streetbrand.com*

As well as tips on how to prepare for, and conduct yourself at, the interview itself this book has examples of the kind of answers interviewers really want to hear; the kind of answers that will get you that job. And if you can't find the answer to the question you want the author invites you to email it to him and he'll send an answer!

ISBN 978-1-84528-238-7

HOW TO SUCCEED AT INTERVIEWS
DR ROB YEUNG

'To be interviewed without having read it is an opportunity missed.' *Sunday Times*

'*How To Succeed at Interviews* is the type of book that one may not wish to share with others who are job seeking in competition with oneself.'
S Lewis, Coventry

'. . . an invaluable source of information for job hunters on preparing for interviews, tests and assessment centres.'
Jonathan Turpin, Chief Executive, fish4jobs.co.uk

'This is an excellent book; good value ... buy it.'
V Tilbury, Cranfield University

'An engaging read packed with useful observations and tips for job seekers of all ages.'
Roddy Gow, Chairman, Odgers, Ray & Berndtson

ISBN 978-1-84528-259-2

How To Books are available through all good bookshops, or you can order direct from us through Grantham Book Services.

Tel: +44 (0)1476 541080
Fax: +44 (0)1476 541061
Email: orders@gbs.tbs-ltd.co.uk

Or via our website

www.howtobooks.co.uk

To order via any of these methods please quote the title(s) of the book(s) and your credit card number together with its expiry date.

For further information about our books and catalogue, please contact:

How To Books
Spring Hill House
Spring Hill Road
Begbroke
Oxford OX5 1RX

Visit our web site at

www.howtobooks.co.uk

Or you can contact us by email at info@howtobooks.co.uk